THE HORIZON BURNS

A TALE OF SALT, FIRE, AND FIRST CONTACT

RUDRA IYER

Made with ❤ on the Notion Press Platform
www.notionpress.com

For the ones who choose the sea,

even when they are told to stay ashore.

Preface

We write to map the uncharted. Not all frontiers are drawn in ink. Some exist where parchment curls at the edge, where the compass spins aimlessly, and where no name has been etched. Not for lack of wonder, but for lack of witness.

Some lands are mapped instead in salt. In silence. In the soft, stubborn defiance of a boy who chooses the sea.

This story began with a question:

What does it mean to belong, when you come from nowhere?

Not in lineage, not in title. But in the bones, in the breath, in the quiet ache to matter.

Set against the backdrop of the first Portuguese voyage to India, *Where the Map Ends* is not Vasco da Gama's tale. His name is remembered. His voyages charted. His statues still stand. But history is not only shaped by the men who commanded the ships. It is also shaped by those who swabbed their decks.

This is Tomas's story.

A ship's boy. An orphan. A runaway with nothing to lose but the chains of Lisbon's alleys. A boy forgotten by the land, and perhaps, remembered by the sea.

This novel is fiction. But it was born from truth. The kind buried deep in footnotes, behind grand victories and inked names. It is inspired by the invisible: the carpenters who patched torn sails, the cooks who stoked fire in iron bellies, the wide-eyed boys who learned the shape of the world not from books, but from bruises and storms.

These are the lives history forgets. And yet, perhaps the sea remembers. And perhaps fiction, like the sea, allows them to rise again.

Acknowledgements

My deepest gratitude to the storytellers who sail before me, especially those who taught me to listen to silence and salt. To my parents, thank you for your fierce encouragement and tireless feedback.

To the voices from history who never got their due: this one is for you.

Disclaimer

This is a work of fiction. While it draws inspiration from real historical figures and events, liberties have been taken to serve the narrative. Any resemblance to actual persons, living or dead, is coincidental and unintended, except where explicitly stated. The cultures and geographies portrayed are interpreted through a fictional lens.

Prologue: Where the Map Ends

Lisbon, Portugal, Winter, 1497

It was a cold, grey evening in Lisbon. The clouds were low and thick, hinting at rain that hadn't yet come. Daylight was slipping away behind the rooftops, leaving the harbour in a kind of gloom.

Down at the docks, the smell of tar mixed with seawater. Timber creaked under the weight of cargo. Men moved between crates and ropes, tired, quiet, and bundled against the chill. Their faces told stories of long weeks without rest, of meals missed, and coins stretched too thin.

The ships waited at anchor, rising and falling with the tide. Their sails were tied up tight, barely moving in the breeze. Now and then, a strip of canvas would flap and snap, sharp in the silence. A seagull let out a harsh cry above and disappeared into the clouds.

At the edge of the quay, a man stood still, away from the others. His cloak was worn and heavy. Salt stains lined its edges, and the leather underneath looked like it had seen too many storms. His beard was thick and black. His eyes were fixed on the ships.

Vasco da Gama.

He didn't speak. He just looked at the fleet: the *Sao Gabriel*, the *Sao Rafael*, and the *Berrio*, the three ships that would carry him toward the unknown. He was weighing something. Maybe the weather. Maybe the journey ahead. Or maybe the weight of everything he had promised to deliver.

Behind him, the city crawled under the weight of winter; grey roofs, narrow alleys, smoke rising from hovels where bread was a blessing. Lisbon, like all of Portugal, waited. For gold. For glory. For God.

The Whisper of the East

In the halls of the royal palace, warm with tapestries and incense, a different kind of storm brewed. King Manuel I sat draped in velvet and fatigue. He was thirty-five, a man too young to be wearied, but wearied still. By maps, by merchants, by war, and by the looming shadow of Spain.

Before him, spread like a game board, lay the known world. Europe, Africa, the Atlantic, and then, at the edge of the parchment, sketched in fading ink: *India*.

"Terra dos especiarias."

Land of spices.

A world whispered about in the corridors of Venice, promised in Arabian tales, smuggled in sacks of pepper and cinnamon that fetched more than silver. A world that had eluded them for centuries.

Manuel leaned forward.

"Find me that land, and Portugal will never kneel to Castile again." The bishop beside him, pale and severe, crossed himself.

"Find it, Your Majesty, and you will bring the Cross to heathen kings."

The court was divided between merchants who hungered, and priests who feared. Some warned of heresies beyond the Cape of Good Hope. Others, of demons that guarded the edge of the sea. There were no charts, only whispers. No certainty, only the glimmer of gold.

And so they turned to Vasco da Gama. A quiet man with a ruthless streak and no love for courtiers. He was not a diplomat. He was a storm in human form.

The Prophet of Dust

Two nights before departure, a monk from Santarem rode into Lisbon. His robe was torn at the hem, and his sandals caked with frost. He asked no permission, offered no greeting. Just stormed into the royal chapel, eyes wild with dust and God.

He spoke in Latin and riddles.

"The sea will open its mouth and take what it pleases," he cried. "The East is fire, and those who chase it will burn!"

The bishop called for silence. But King Manuel, superstitious and cunning, listened. "Speak plainly, friar."

The monk trembled. "You send men into the ocean to chase the sun. But beyond the sun waits a land of many gods, where incense blinds and gold deceives. You seek wealth, but you may find ruin. Or worse; enchantment."

The court scoffed.

But later that night, Manuel wrote in his own hand: *Let da Gama be warned, but not restrained. A fire may light the way, even if it burns.*

A Prayer for the Damned

At the Monastery of Jeronimos, a hush fell. The sailors, cloaked in wool and fear, knelt beneath vaulted ceilings carved like forest canopies. Candles shivered in the wind. A priest read aloud from the Book of Psalms.

"Though I walk through the valley of the shadow of death, I shall fear no evil..."

Da Gama stood apart. He did not kneel. His mind was not on Psalms, but on the cargo manifest.

Still, when the priest offered holy water, he did not refuse. Salt and faith; both were needed for voyages such as this.

Around him, the crew ranged from veterans with empty purses to boys who had never seen the ocean. The youngest looked barely fifteen. Some prayed. Some wept. All of them would soon sail beyond where any European had dared.

They called the voyage *A Cruzada das Especiarias*. The Crusade of Spices.

But it was not God who drove them.

It was pepper. Cinnamon. Cloves. Silk.

It was stories of cities where the streets gleamed with saffron, where kings rode elephants, and even the air smelled sweet.

India.

No one had seen it. But they all dreamed of it.

Where the Map Ends

Three days before sailing, an old cartographer from Sagres was summoned to the palace. He brought a single, tattered scroll, yellowed and smudged with ink.

He rolled it open, and there it was: the edge of Africa, the southern curve, the Cape of Storms. And then... nothing.

"This is where the map ends," he whispered. "Beyond this, no Christian man has gone." The King stared at the blank parchment. "Then we must draw new lines."

Vasco da Gama did not speak. He only stared at that white space. That abyss. That promise. He saw no monsters. No devils. Only wind. And salt. And fire.

Three weeks later, the fleet would round the Cape. Ten months later, they would reach Calicut.

And one boy; who had not yet stepped aboard, would witness a world that would change him forever.

But that was still to come.

For now, the sails were furled. The ocean was black. And the map had ended.

CHAPTER ONE

The Boy Who Chose the Sea

Lisbon, Portugal, Winter, 1497

The pungent aroma of boiled cabbage and coal dust lingered in the alleyways like a bad dream. Smoke curled up lazily from crooked chimneys. Rats darted between puddles slick with piss and rain. In the workers' quarter of Lisbon, even the wind seemed tired.

Tomas bent over the tannery vat, his hands red and raw. The water stung worse in winter. His fingers had cracked weeks ago, and now they bled slowly, quietly, like they'd given up complaining.

"Faster, dog!"

A voice snapped like a whip. Mestre Joao. Fat-bellied. Sweat-soaked. His teeth stained brown from chewing cloves. He stood above the vats, arms folded, eyes sharp.

Tomas flinched. His back ached from bending. His legs were numb. Still, he dunked another hide into the bitter liquid, the fumes choking his throat.

"If you're too weak for honest work," Mestre Joao sneered, stepping closer, "I'll sell you to the ships. They always need rats to swab decks and die quietly."

Tomas didn't answer. He didn't look up. Looking up meant catching a cuff to the jaw.

He'd heard of the ships. Everyone had. Big, creaking monsters with sails like wings. The king had ordered them to sail beyond the end of the world. That's what they said in the streets. Beyond the map. To the East. To lands where gold grew on trees and spices danced on the tongue. Cinnamon. Clove. Pepper. Words that tasted better than food.

Sometimes, Tomas dreamed of those places. When sleep came, which wasn't often.

That night, he stole a crust of bread from the tannery's kitchen and climbed the hill behind the quarter. From there, you could just make out the masts in the harbour. Tall, still shadows under a thin moon.

Tomas sat on a cold rock and chewed slowly. The bread was hard, dry enough to scrape his throat. But it was warm in his hands, and for once, no one shouted at him.

A cough startled him. He saw an old man leaning against a tree stump, wrapped in a ragged cloak, breath steaming up in the air. The man's nose was crooked, like it had been broken twice. He cradled a wineskin in his hands.

"Beautiful, aren't they?" the man rasped in a gravelly voice, nodding toward the harbour. Tomas didn't speak. He chewed and waited.

The old man chuckled. "I sailed once. Before the bones got lazy. Seen the coast of Africa. Tasted dates fresh from the trees. Danced with a girl who wore nothing but gold rings."

Tomas raised an eyebrow. The man grinned.

"They're going farther this time. Past the Cape. Eastward. All the way to India, they say. Land of gods and fire and jewels you can eat."

India. Tomas had heard the name whispered, always with wonder. A place drawn on no map he'd ever seen.

"You thinking of going?" the old man asked, squinting. Tomas looked away. "They don't take boys like me."

"No," the man agreed. "They don't. But boys like you take themselves."

The next morning, Mestre Joao beat him.

He didn't say why. He didn't need a reason. His hands were fists before the sun rose, and Tomas was the closest thing. By noon, Tomas's lip was split and his ribs screamed with every breath. He worked through it. The hides waited.

That night, Tomas didn't go back to the hill. He scuttled through the narrow alleys of Alfama, each step slick with the slime of discarded fish and winter slush.

His breath came out in clouds, but he didn't feel the cold. Not anymore. He only felt the sting where Mestre Joao's stick had cracked across his back, still burning through the coarse wool of his tunic.

He ducked beneath a crumbling archway where stray cats huddled. They scattered at the sight of him, as if they too had learned to fear the quick, angry steps of working men.

He pressed his back against the cold wall, heart thudding. His hands trembled, not from fear, but from rage. For two years he had endured Joao's blows, the endless days of labor in the shipyard, the sneers of men who saw him as nothing more than an orphaned stray with no family, no future. He had eaten what the rats left behind. Slept in corners the wind forgot. Dreamed of a life that didn't smell of pitch and rot.

And now, he had done it. He had struck back. Not with a fist, but with eyes that did not look down. With a stare that said, *No more.*

He clutched the canvas satchel tight to his chest, his entire life packed into a bag no bigger than a baker's loaf. A broken comb. A half-carved bird he had whittled by candlelight. A silver coin he had stolen from a drunk sailor six months ago and never spent.

Tomas turned toward the sea.

Down at the docks, the lanterns flickered against the wind, their yellow light reflected in puddles. The ships moored there looked like sleeping giants, draped in shadow and rope. Sailors moved about like ghosts, hunched and muttering, their faces hidden under hoods and beards.

He spotted the fleet right away. The three ships had an air about them, cleaner, prouder. Their hulls polished with fresh tar, sails tucked away like folded wings. Each had a name carved into her side: *Sao Gabriel*, *Sao Rafael*, and *Berrio.*

He had heard the whispers. Everyone in the yard had. A voyage beyond the known world. To a land of gold and spice. Where even the air smelled sweet, and men drank from cups made of ivory.

A voyage led by Vasco da Gama himself. The king's man. The explorer. The one who had stood before Prince Manuel and asked for ships to chase the edge of the world.

Tomas moved closer, crouching behind crates. He scanned the deck of the *Sao Rafael*, searching for a way in. A way *up.*

A boy his age, maybe younger, ran down the gangplank, dragging a coil of rope. He wore a sailor's cap and had a thin frame. Tomas recognised the quick shuffle of an errand boy. If that lad could be aboard, why not him?

Tomas crept closer to the supply ramp where crates of salted pork, barrels of vinegar, and sacks of dried beans were being hauled up under the torchlight.

"Oi! You there!" a voice barked. Tomas froze.

A squat man with arms like tree trunks approached. His cheeks were red with cold, and a knife glinted at his belt.

"I ain't seen you before. You got papers?"

Tomas licked his lips, thinking fast. "I'm with the stevedores," he lied. "Sent to help with the night load."

The man narrowed his eyes. "At this hour? Don't take me for a goat." Tomas held his gaze. "Captain's orders."

The man grunted. "Get in line, then. And if I catch you thieving, I'll gut you like mackerel." Tomas nodded and slipped past, his heart pounding.

He worked through the next hour hauling sacks. Heavy, back-breaking work. But he didn't complain. He needed to blend in. Every lifted barrel was a step closer to escape. To something *new*.

When the shift changed and the dock quieted, Tomas ducked into the shadows and made for the hold of the *Sao Rafael*. He found a gap between barrels near the stern and curled up in it, wrapping his arms around his knees.

He didn't sleep. He listened. To the creak of rope, the murmur of waves, the whistle of the wind in the sails not yet raised.

He whispered into the dark, "God, if You are watching, let this work. I don't want to die in Alfama. Let me see the land where cinnamon grows."

He didn't know if anyone heard.

But the tide was rising. And the ships would leave with the morning.

When dawn came, the crew stirred like bees in a shaken hive. Men shouted. Ropes slapped the deck. A bell rang three times. Sails unfurled slowly, catching the cold wind like sighs.

Tomas peered from his hiding place.

Then, he heard the voice that would change his life.

"Check the hold," came the order. "No stowaways. Captain's orders." Boots on wood. Closer. Too close.

Tomas held his breath.

A sailor yanked back the tarp over the barrels. His eyes met Tomas's. "What's this, then?"

Tomas sat up, heart thudding. "I can work," he blurted. "Strong back, quiet mouth. Please." The sailor stared at him, then called over his shoulder. "Found a rat with a tongue."

More boots. A shadow loomed. A tall man with a trimmed beard, sharp eyes, and a long coat stepped forward. He did not speak at once. He only looked.

"Your name?" "Tomas," he whispered. "Why are you here?"

"I don't want to die in the gutters of Lisbon. I want..., I want to see the edge of the world."

The man said nothing for a moment. Then he turned to the sailor. "We'll need more hands. Put him to work. If he slacks, throw him overboard."

Tomas exhaled. He didn't smile. Not yet. But something inside him, something small and stubborn, began to burn.

He had chosen the sea. And the sea, it seemed, had chosen him back.

CHAPTER TWO

Salt in the Wound

The first morning at sea was not like the stories he'd clung to as a boy. No bold captains beneath fluttering sails, no salt-kissed sunrises or soaring gulls to guide the way. Only cold wind and the smell of sickness.

Tomas had risen before the bell, if he had slept at all. The planks beneath him creaked like bones. Everything was damp: his clothes, his skin, the very air. It smelled of pitch, brine, and men who hadn't washed in days.

He stepped onto the main deck as a stranger, the sky above still the colour of old steel. Men grunted as they hauled rope, scoured decks, and shouted half-words into the wind. No one looked at him.

Not yet.

But he watched them. Their hands like knotted rope, faces hardened from years of salt and sun. They worked as though the ship was an extension of their body. No wasted movement. Every pull had purpose.

"Eh, rat," came a bark from behind. "This ain't no theatre. You want a show, dive overboard and juggle sharks. You're crew now, earn your breath."

It was the same broad-shouldered sailor who'd found him in the hold. His name, Tomas learned, was Martim. Older than most, with eyes that had seen too much and lips always curled around a splinter of straw.

Martim threw a coil of rope at Tomas's feet. "You know how to tie a knot?" Tomas hesitated, then bent down. His fingers fumbled with the coarse line. Martim snorted. "By the saints, we're doomed."

That morning, Tomas scrubbed the deck till his palms bled. He swabbed piss and puke from corners the sun never reached. He carried barrels of water with a yoke across his shoulders that bit into his skin. Every few steps, he was cursed at. Shoved. Corrected.

He didn't speak much. When he did, his Portuguese sounded like cracked clay among the smoother Lisbon accents.

"Boy's from Alfama," one sailor said. "They're born with fish guts in their teeth." "Aye," another added, "and rats in their bed."

They laughed. Tomas did not react. But in his mind, he measured them all.

By evening, the fleet was far from the shore. The land a thin memory behind mist. The sea stretched in all directions, blue, black, and endless.

He leaned over the railing, sick from the rolling belly of the ship. His ribs ached. His tongue tasted of bile and regret. The sea stretched on, a dark joke with no punchline.

A voice beside him said, "Don't fight it. Breathe with your mouth. Like this."

Tomas turned. A boy about his age stood there, red hair under a salt-crusted cap. His nose was too big for his face, and he had the kind of smile that made it hard to stay angry.

"I'm Diogo," the boy said. "Cook's runner. You're the stowaway, eh?"

Tomas nodded, wiping his mouth.

Diogo leaned back against the rail. "My first voyage too. Thought I'd see whales. Maybe mermaids. All I've seen is vomit."

That earned a small laugh from Tomas. "You got a bunk?" Diogo asked.

"I sleep by the barrels."

"Cold there. Come find me tomorrow. I'll show you a place near the galley pipes. Warmer."

That night, Tomas lay curled beside barrels of salted meat. The cold seeped into his bones, but he remembered Diogo's grin. It made the dark a little smaller.

Life aboard the *Sao Rafael* was a rhythm of suffering and strange beauty.

The ship groaned and creaked like a living thing. Ropes hissed. Sails snapped. The hull spoke in whispers at night.

Tomas learned to wake with the bell, to eat fast, work faster. He learned to wrap rags around his hands before hauling rope. To duck when the bosun shouted. To step lightly over the slick boards or risk losing teeth to a wave.

He cleaned pots in the galley, where Diogo tossed him scrap, bread crusts, fish eyes, once even a slice of orange. He swallowed them like jewels.

"You ever eat orange before?" Diogo asked once. Tomas shook his head. "Never even seen one till now."

Diogo looked amazed. "They come from down south. Where the earth is red and trees bleed sap. You'll see."

Tomas didn't dare hope. But he remembered the taste for days.

The days bled together, broken only by the changing sky. Tomas grew to recognise weather by scent and sound. A yellowish horizon meant storms. A still sea meant trouble. Once, lightning flickered on the edge of a squall for hours, never striking, like a beast pacing the confines of a cage in the clouds.

Nights were worst. The cold wind gnawed through his threadbare cloak. The stars above mocked him while he rocked endlessly below.

One night, he listened to the carpenter sing to himself while mending a cracked spar. It was a haunting tune, soft and wordless, passed down from some coastal village. Tomas didn't know the words, but the melody lodged in him.

Sometimes the men told stories; of sea serpents longer than the ship, of ghost ships with white sails that hunted in fog. Tomas listened silently, eyes wide, soaking it all.

But he also learned the price of error.

It happened in the third week. He was told to secure a line. A simple enough task, he thought. But he looped it wrong. When the wind rose, the knot slipped. A sail cracked loose, nearly snapping the mast. The ship reeled. Men shouted.

Martim stormed over, grabbed him by the collar, and dragged him forward.

"See this rope?" he growled. "You tie it wrong again, and it won't be a sail that tears. It'll be you." He struck Tomas once, open palm, hard. Not cruelly. Not like Mestre Joao. But it stung all the same. Later, Diogo found him crouched beside the chicken crates.

"Martim's not the worst," Diogo said. "He just wants to stay alive." Tomas nodded.

He remembered the tannery. The stink of boiling hides. The lash of the master's belt. The way boys disappeared after fevers. Here, the pain had a shape. A reason. It was different.

Here, he was part of something.

He began to learn names. There was Old Joan, who patched sails and spat black tobacco. Henrique, who kept a pet rat in his sleeve. Pires, who carved tiny ships from driftwood and prayed to every saint he knew before eating. And above them all, the first mate, Vitor, silent as a blade, who watched Tomas sometimes with unreadable eyes.

They taught him, some kindly, others roughly. How to hoist the mizzen, clean the bilge, carry water without spilling. How to make himself useful without getting in the way.

There was a storm one evening. Not fierce, but enough to make the ship dance. Barrels rolled loose. A man broke a tooth. Tomas held a lantern steady while Diogo scrambled to save the cooking knives. That night, they laughed so hard their ribs ached.

He began to understand. The ship was a world. Its own rules. Its own gods.

That night, he dreamt of cinnamon trees and rivers of gold. Of warm sun on his back and names spoken with respect. The next morning, he tied the knot right; tight, clean, and dreaming.

As days drifted on, Tomas and Diogo grew closer. It wasn't the closeness of kinship, but of shared hardship. Two souls thrown together by fate, enduring the same biting winds, the same unrelenting demands of the ship. They were different in many ways. Diogo had a sharp wit and an easy manner, whereas Tomas was quiet, pensive, slow to trust. But the bond between them was undeniable, forged in the fires of salt and sweat.

One morning, Tomas found himself standing with Diogo beside the galley, their arms resting on the railing as they watched the horizon break into light. The air was damp, thick with mist, the kind that clung to the skin like damp rags. The ship rocked gently, as if lulled by the quiet of the sea.

"So," Diogo said, a teasing lilt in his voice, "you've seen a whale yet?" Tomas shook his head. "Not yet."

"Ah, you will," Diogo continued, with the certainty of someone who believed in the world's hidden wonders. "They come at night, mostly, when the moon is full. They rise from the depths like spirits."

Tomas smiled, despite himself. "Spirits?"

"Aye. Giant, ancient ones. You'll see them dance beneath the waves. Like kings of the sea." Diogo leaned forward, eyes bright. "But you have to be awake to see them."

Tomas nodded. He wasn't sure if he believed in the whales, but there was a magic to Diogo's words. An infectious spark that made the ship seem less like a prison and more like an adventure.

Days merged into weeks. The routine became a rhythm that Tomas's body learned to obey without thought. He rose with the bell at dawn, worked until the sun dipped below the horizon, and then collapsed into sleep in the cramped quarters beneath the deck. The ship was always moving, always groaning under the pressure of the sea, but it was a strange comfort. The steady sway, the creaking of timbers—it was predictable. Unlike the tannery, where every moment had felt heavy with the threat of violence or hardship.

One evening, as the sun dipped low and the sea began to shimmer with a golden hue, Diogo approached Tomas with an impish grin. "The men are meeting by the aft tonight," he said in a conspiratorial whisper. "It's a ritual. Sailor's luck, you know?"

Tomas raised an eyebrow, intrigued. He had learned enough by now to know that sailors had a thousand little rituals, some of which bordered on the absurd, while others held a deep, unspoken meaning for them.

"What is it?" Tomas asked.

"A drink. A prayer. A few words to the sea gods," Diogo said. "And maybe some stories, if you're lucky. But tonight, we do something special. You'll see."

Later, as the bell rang to signal the end of the workday, Tomas followed Diogo to the aft, where a small group of men had gathered. Old Joan was there, a pipe dangling from his lips. Henrique stood with a rat perched on his shoulder, whispering something to it. Pires, the silent woodcarver, sat cross-legged on the deck, his hands moving deftly over a new piece of driftwood. The men were all wearing worn-out, mismatched clothes, but there was a sense of unity in the way they stood together.

Diogo handed Tomas a cup, filled with a clear, foul-smelling liquid. "Drink," he said. "It's for luck."

Tomas took the cup hesitantly, sniffing it. The smell made his stomach turn, but he trusted Diogo and raised it to his lips. The liquid burned like fire, scorching down his throat, and he fought the urge to gag.

"Saints above," Tomas muttered, wiping his mouth.

The men laughed. "Good lad," said Henrique, the one with the rat, his voice full of mirth. "You've survived the first test."

"And now," Joan said, his voice gruff but kind, "we offer a prayer."

The sailors bowed their heads and murmured low, guttural words. Tomas could not understand them. They were prayers to the sea gods, to the winds, to the stars that guided them through the dark. The words felt ancient, older than the ship, older than the men themselves.

When the prayer was finished, Diogo stood, raising his cup in the air. "To the sea, and to those who sail upon it!" he said, and the men cheered.

Tomas, still feeling the burn of the drink in his belly, joined them. He didn't know the names of the gods they worshipped, but there was something in the ritual that made him feel connected to them. Something in the air that hummed with a kind of ancient power.

The evening wore on, and the men began telling stories. Some were funny, others dark, but all of them were steeped in the salt and blood of the sea. Tomas listened, his mind drifting between the words, between the creaks of the ship and the sound of the waves.

"There was once a ship," Joan began, "that went out from Lisbon, much like this one. But they were caught in a storm—a storm that had no end."

"What happened to them?" Tomas asked, leaning forward.

"Nothing," Joan said, his voice low. "They vanished. The ship, the crew, all of it. And now, they say, if you listen closely enough at night, you can hear their cries. Those lost at sea."

The mood grew heavy, and Tomas could feel the weight of their words settle over him. He glanced at Diogo, but the boy's face was unreadable. He had heard the stories before, no doubt.

The ritual ended with the men heading back to their posts, but Tomas felt something linger in the air. There was power in these traditions, power in their beliefs, even if he didn't fully understand it.

As the days went on, Tomas's bond with Diogo deepened. They shared food when they could, swapped stories of their lives before the ship, and laughed at the absurdity of their situation. Tomas learned that Diogo had been a cook's runner for years, always moving from ship to ship, never staying long enough to put down roots. He had seen ports from one end of the world to the other, though he spoke little of his past.

But Tomas, too, had stories. He shared the bitter memories of the tannery—the stench of the hides, the lash of the master's belt, the endless hours spent in the heat, working like an animal. He told Diogo about the people he'd known, the friends he'd lost, and the hunger that gnawed at him like a beast.

Diogo listened without judgment, nodding occasionally, offering a few words of comfort. Tomas didn't need much—just someone to hear him, someone who understood what it meant to live in the shadows of the world.

One afternoon, as the ship sailed under a sky painted in shades of red and orange, Diogo leaned against the mast and spoke in a voice quieter than usual.

"Do you ever think about what's next, Tomas?" he asked, his eyes distant.

Tomas paused, feeling the weight of the question settle in his chest. "What do you mean?" "I mean..." Diogo hesitated. "After this voyage. What happens when we get there?"

Tomas thought about it. The truth was, he hadn't given much thought to the end of the journey. He had only cared about surviving the next day, the next hour.

"I don't know," Tomas said at last. "I just want something better than what I left behind."

"Maybe you'll find it," Diogo said, giving him a grin. "But you have to look for it, Tomas. You can't just wait for it to come to you."

Tomas nodded. He didn't know if Diogo was right, but for the first time since he had stepped onto the ship, he felt the stirrings of something more than just survival. It was hope, fragile and fleeting, but it was there.

And so, Tomas continued to work, continued to learn, and continued to hope. Each day brought new challenges, new rituals, and new friendships. He was no longer the lost boy from Alfama, the one who had boarded the ship out of desperation. He was becoming something else. Something more.

As the days passed, the sea seemed less a prison and more a vast, unknowable realm. Tomas was no longer just surviving. He was living. And in that living, he had found something he never thought he would: a chance at something more.

The ship creaked beneath him, and Tomas, his hands calloused, his mind restless, looked out over the endless expanse of the sea. The horizon stretched before him, as if beckoning him toward something new.

And for the first time, he didn't mind that he didn't know what it was.

CHAPTER THREE

The Weight of the Horizon

The days blurred into one another like the endless sea.

Tomas had grown used to the creaks and groans of the *Sao Rafael.* The endless sway of the ship, the pitch of the sails, the damp air that clung to his skin. It all became a part of him. A rhythm, even a comfort. But there were moments when the weight of it; the open water stretching far beyond what he could see, the vast nothingness that surrounded them, pressed on him like a stone, a heavy weight on his chest.

He found himself staring at the horizon often, lost in the line where the sea kissed the sky. It was never the same. Sometimes it was a jagged, angry line of black clouds. Other times, a soft curve of gold in the morning sun. But always, it was a reminder of how small he was.

How insignificant.

Diogo, too, spent long stretches of the day at the rail, but always with a faraway look in his eyes, a smile still easy on his lips. The boy was a puzzle. He had stories of faraway lands, strange creatures, and adventures that seemed more myth than reality. And yet, there was a sadness to him, a quiet ache that Tomas could not place.

The two of them had become inseparable. They ate together, worked together, even shared a small space under the galley pipes, where the warmth from the cooking fires made the nights bearable.

It was a simple life. But it was life, and it was new. Tomas thought about the tannery only in flashes now. The stench of the hides. The sting of the master's lash. The hollow days spent in the gloom.

But it was still there, lurking beneath everything. He had never fully left it behind. "You there! Boy!"

Tomas turned. A tall man with a face like carved stone and a cloak that snapped in the wind stood above him on the quarterdeck. Tomas had seen him before; the captain's second, called Fernao. He spoke little, but his eyes missed nothing.

"Yes, senhor?" Tomas straightened. "You've been watching the sea."

"I have."

"Why?"

Tomas blinked. No one had ever asked him a question without expecting a lie in return. "I was trying to see if the edge is real."

Fernao's mouth twitched, not quite a smile. "You think we'll fall off?" "I don't know," Tomas said honestly.

The officer stared at him a moment longer. Then he turned and descended the steps. "Report to the sail master. He's short a hand."

Tomas ran. Not from fear. But from the rare joy of being seen.

The sail master, Senhor Agular, was a man of ropes and swears. His hands were always coated in pitch and his sentences never ended without a threat. But he taught well. And Tomas, despite the ache in his arms and the endless bruises, learned quickly.

"How do you tie a cleat hitch, boy?" "Like this, senhor."

"Faster next time. If the wind shifts while you're fumbling, it'll snap the mast and take your head with it."

"Yes, senhor."

The days passed not in hours, but in tasks. When the sky was pale and the wind behaved, they sang. When the waves rose like angry gods, they did not speak, only held on and prayed.

Once, during a quiet evening, Tomas found himself beside a man named Joao Pereira, a sailor with one eye and a tattoo of Saint Elmo on his forearm. For a while, Tomas was reminded of his old master. But this man was very different.

"You got the look of a land rat," Joao grunted. "But the sea hasn't eaten you yet." "It tries," Tomas said.

Joao chuckled. "Aye. It always does." "Have you ever seen it?" Tomas asked. "Seen what?"

"The edge."

Joao looked at him, the lines in his weathered face softening. "Boy, the sea has no edge. It only has appetite. It gives, then it takes. And it always asks for more than you think you owe."

One evening, the sky darkened with the promise of a storm. The wind had begun to howl, and the air felt thick with anticipation. Tomas stood beside Diogo, holding onto the railing as the ship rocked with the increasing waves.

"We're going to see it," Diogo said, his voice raised above the wind. His eyes sparkled with excitement, but Tomas could see the nervousness underneath. "The big one. The storm of the season."

"Is it... bad?" Tomas asked, his throat dry.

Diogo grinned, showing a flash of teeth. "You've heard the stories. It's going to tear us apart, and then some. But we'll survive. We're sailors, aren't we?"

Tomas didn't respond. He had heard the stories. Of the storms that could split a ship in half, of the waves that could swallow whole men. He hadn't signed up for this. He had come for the freedom, for the adventure. But he hadn't known what that truly meant.

The ship's crew moved with a practiced ease, pulling in ropes, securing the sails, and preparing for the worst. Tomas watched them, awe and fear stirring in his chest.

"Do you think we'll make it through?" Tomas asked.

Diogo's gaze softened, and for a moment, Tomas saw the boy he had come to trust; the one who had shared his first piece of orange, who had shown him the warmth of the galley pipes.

"I think we will," Diogo said softly. "But it's not the storm we need to worry about. It's the men." Tomas frowned. "What do you mean?"

"Men change when the storm comes. They forget who they are. Some fight it, some run from it. And some; they let it take them."

Tomas didn't fully understand, but he nodded. In the darkening hours, there wasn't much to say. The storm came in the dead of night.

It hit without warning, like a beast waking from a long slumber. The wind screamed like a banshee. Waves taller than the ship itself crashed against the hull, sending spray over the sides. The deck tilted violently, and Tomas had to grab onto the nearest rope to keep from being thrown into the sea.

The crew worked in a frenzy. The first mate, Vitor, shouted orders, his voice cutting through the chaos like a blade. Tomas couldn't see him through the sheets of rain, but he could feel his presence, like a force of nature. He was there, at the heart of the storm, unshaken, guiding them all.

Tomas held onto the rope, his knuckles white, his heart hammering in his chest. This was real. This was the sea he had dreamed of. The raw, untamed power that could crush him in an instant.

Through the howling winds, Tomas heard a voice beside him.

"Stay close," Diogo shouted, his face grim. "Hold on tight. Don't let go."

The boy's voice was steady, but his hands trembled slightly. Tomas nodded, and together, they braced against the storm, their bodies pressed to the railing as the ship pitched and rocked. The ship groaned and creaked, as if it, too, was fighting for its life.

Tomas thought about the tannery again. About the certainty of its misery. How everything was predictable, and yet, there was nothing to hold onto. The storm was wild, unpredictable, but it felt more alive than anything he had known.

He didn't know which was worse: the storm itself or the fear that it stirred in him.

Hours passed, and Tomas lost all sense of time. His arms ached from holding onto the rope, his legs burned from bracing against the ship's violent movements. But he never let go. Not once.

Finally, the storm began to wane. The winds eased. The waves lessened. The ship still rocked, but it was a gentler roll now. The sea, though still wild, seemed less angry, less threatening.

The crew began to move more cautiously, checking for damage, repairing the sails, and pulling in the ropes. Vitor stood at the helm, his eyes narrow, scanning the horizon.

Tomas exhaled a breath he didn't realise he had been holding. He looked at Diogo, who was already grinning, his teeth flashing white in the pale light.

"Well, that wasn't so bad, eh?" Diogo said.

Tomas didn't answer right away. His heart was still racing, his breath coming in short gasps. But he couldn't help it. He smiled.

"We made it," Tomas said. His voice sounded small, but it was enough.

The next few days were quieter. The sea had calmed, the skies had cleared, and the ship moved steadily towards the unknown. Tomas found himself back at the railing, watching the horizon, though it no longer held the same fear it once did.

He had learned something about himself during the storm. Something that had been buried deep inside him, hidden under years of hard work and survival. He wasn't afraid of the sea anymore. Not in the way he had been before.

But the storm had changed him. It had carved a space in him where something new had begun to grow. Something that was bigger than fear, bigger than survival. Hope, maybe. Or maybe it was just a sense of purpose.

Either way, he wasn't the same boy who had boarded this ship weeks ago.

Tomas had seen the way the crew had come together, how they moved as one, a unit in the face of the storm. And he understood now that he, too, was part of that. He was no longer the stowaway, the outsider. He was part of the *Sao Rafael*.

And maybe, just maybe, he was starting to believe that he belonged.

One night, as the moon hung low and red, the men gathered near the mainmast for a reading. The captain himself stood before them. Vasco da Gama, tall and calm, his beard trimmed, his eyes sharp.

"We follow in the wake of Bartolomeu Dias," he said. "But we sail farther. We seek India. We seek a passage others have only dreamed of. We are the hands of the crown, the breath of Portugal. And we will not fail."

The men cheered. Tomas did not. He watched. And for the first time, he saw that da Gama was not simply a man. He was a figure carved from intent. A storm given the shape of human flesh. And Tomas, hiding at the edge of the circle, knew: this man would take them to the edge. And perhaps beyond it.

He whispered to the stars, "Let me live long enough to see it."

The stars did not answer. But the sails above them shifted, caught by a sudden wind. And the ship moved forward.

Weeks passed. The ships rounded the Cape Verde Islands, stopping to refill barrels with rainwater and salted meat. The air grew warmer. The winds turned kinder. Flying fish burst from the water in silver arcs. Nights no longer bit with cold, but embraced with a breathless heat that left sweat in every fold.

Tomas grew sun-dark and wind-lean. His hands no longer cracked. His footing grew sure. And in his chest, something began to settle. Not comfort. But belonging.

He was not a sailor yet. But he was no longer a stranger to the sea.

CHAPTER FOUR

The Horizon Burns

They sighted land on the seventeenth day.

At first it was a smear of greenish grey on the horizon, rising like a bruise from the sea. Then, as the ship crept closer, the contours sharpened: jagged cliffs, a thin strip of beach, and behind it, the wild interior of Sao Tome. The sky above boiled with a tropical haze, clouds stacked high like white fortresses, light slashing between them in spears.

Tomas stood at the prow, wind lashing his face. Around him, the crew buzzed with renewed energy. Shirts were straightened. Beards combed. Boots polished, or at least scraped clean of rot. After weeks of salt and sky, the promise of land felt unreal. Like a fable they'd talked themselves into believing.

Diogo nudged him. "Looks like paradise, doesn't it?" Tomas didn't answer. The land felt too quiet. Watching.

The *Sao Rafael* anchored in the sheltered bay by late afternoon. Longboats were lowered with practiced speed. Orders barked. Men scrambled. There was cargo to be inspected, stores to be replenished, and instructions to be received from the port captain. Tomas wasn't assigned to the first boat. He and Diogo stayed aboard, tasked with re-coiling ropes and scrubbing the upper deck.

But the island reached them anyway, through scent.

Flowers, wet earth, smoke from distant fires. Spices so thick on the air Tomas could taste them: cardamom, pepper, nutmeg. It made his stomach twist with hunger and wonder. Compared to the rancid barrels and dried fish, this was a banquet laid out on the wind.

As dusk fell, lanterns bloomed across the shore like low stars. Tomas watched them sway. Fires flickered near the tree line. Somewhere, a drum began to beat, slow, deliberate, like a second heartbeat.

"That sound," Diogo whispered, "isn't just music. It's memory." Tomas looked at him.

"My uncle told me. The people here; they carve history into sound. They don't write books. They make rhythm. Every beat has a story."

He leaned in, lowering his voice.

"My uncle told me about a drum hidden deep in the forest," Diogo said. "Made from the skin of a leopard that only walked under eclipses. They say it was strung tight with the hair of a murdered priest, and every beat it made could summon the past. Not just stories, *sights*. Whole memories. The air would shimmer, and the dead would walk for a moment, repeating what they'd done, exactly as it happened."

Tomas raised an eyebrow.

"Swear it," Diogo grinned. "He said the elders guard it still. They call it *Tambor de Sangue.* The Blood Drum. If you beat it wrong, you summon something that hasn't happened yet. Something that *wants* to happen."

He paused, watching Tomas.

"Last man who tried to steal it, well, they say his ship returned empty. No crew, no blood, just a single drumbeat echoing from the hold every night it floated. No one boards her now. They say she still drifts somewhere south of the island."

The jungle behind the bay rustled faintly in the wind.

Tomas didn't smile. He wasn't entirely sure Diogo was joking anymore.

That night, they slept under the open sky. The deck warm from the day's sun. Tomas dreamt of voices rising from the forest, singing his name. Not chanting, not calling, *singing.* The melody wound through the trees, slipping through leaves and entering his chest like breath.

The next morning, Tomas was part of the second boat crew.

The longboat rocked heavily as they rowed toward shore. The island loomed, lush and steaming, birds darting above the trees. Palm fronds swayed like hands casting spells. A line of black volcanic stone framed the beach, jagged and unnatural, as though the island was warning them off.

"Don't gawk," Martim muttered beside him. "Eyes forward. Hands steady."

They made landfall with a crunch of wet sand. Tomas jumped down, boots sinking into the shore. The heat hit him instantly; a damp, heavy wall. Every breath felt thick, every step louder. Bugs hummed. Crabs scuttled sideways. A dog barked in the distance.

Port Sao Tome unfolded like a painted tapestry. Vivid, chaotic, alive. A scatter of sun-bleached buildings huddled behind palisades of jagged wood, their thatched roofs steaming under the noon blaze. Men of every shade and tongue bustled through the narrow lanes: Moorish merchants in flowing robes, Dutchmen with ruddy cheeks and stiff collars, bare-chested porters with gleaming skin and bright beads around their necks. Barefoot locals moved with quiet grace, balancing baskets brimming with yams, ginger, or salted fish. Women in radiant cloth; reds, ochres, greens like jungle parrots, glided past with clay pots poised like crowns on their heads. The air throbbed with life: bartering voices in a dozen languages, peals of laughter, the call of birds, the steady thrum of drums that seemed to echo from the very earth. It was a place stitched from colour and rhythm, a far cry from Lisbon's gloomy melancholy.

The governor's hut sat at the centre of the compound, raised slightly on a platform of dark timber, its broad roof thick with palm thatch. Faded flags hung limply from a carved beam, and a pair of rusted cannons flanked the entrance like sleeping dogs. Inside, it was cooler, the light filtered through slatted windows and mosquito netting.

Maps curled on the walls. A desk littered with inkwells, ledgers, and sealing wax dominated the room, behind which the governor sat like a spider in its web. Sweating, sunburned, but sharp-eyed. The scent of tobacco, sweat, and sandalwood lingered in the air.

They followed the first mate, Vitor, into the governor's hut. Tomas was told to wait outside. He stood beneath the awning, wiping sweat from his brow, watching a group of children chase a chicken through the dust. A goat bleated from a rooftop. A woman roasted something that smelled like coconut and fish over an open flame.

He didn't know what he expected. But this was't it. This was not the savage wilderness the maps had warned of. Nor was it civilisation as he knew it. It was something else. A world with its own rules, rhythm, memory.

Diogo joined him later, eyes wide with amazement. "Did you see the market? It's like walking through a dream. There's a man selling monkey skulls strung like beads, another with a bird that talks in three languages, and I swear on Saint Elmo's bones, someone was actually eating fire. Just opened his mouth and breathed it, like a dragon in a street show! And the smells Tomas, it's all spice and smoke and fruit. I don't even have names for it!"

Tomas smiled faintly. "What do you think they see when they look at us?" Diogo paused. "Ghosts, maybe. With iron teeth."

Later that afternoon, while helping load timber, Tomas struck up a brief conversation with a sailor named

Henrique. He was older, with a face like weathered bark and tattoos that ran across his knuckles like twisted vines.

"You've got green behind your ears," Henrique said, slapping a beam down. "But you've got good hands."

"Thanks," Tomas said, unsure whether it was a compliment or warning.

Henrique leaned in. "This place... it remembers. Everything you do, it'll echo back to you one day. Remember that when you piss in its rivers or take its fruit."

That evening, they helped haul traded goods back to the ship. Spices in woven sacks that perfumed the air with clove, cinnamon, and star anise; sacks of glossy beans that rattled like treasure; slabs of dark timber wrapped in oilcloth, still damp from the forest, exhaling a rich, loamy scent. One crate broke open, spilling cacao pods. Tomas held one in his hand, rough and warm, like a hardened heart.

"Careful," said a man watching him. He was African; tall, impossibly tall, with skin the colour of burnished mahogany and a presence that seemed to still the air around him. His face was chiseled like a mask from some ancient god's altar: high cheekbones, a proud brow, eyes dark and calm as deep water. Golden rings glinted at his ears, and intricate scars traced quiet stories across his arms. To Tomas, he looked like a figure stepped out of legend. Regal, otherworldly, and utterly at home in this strange, sun-drenched land.

"That's worth more than your weight in gold where you come from."

Tomas nodded. "I've never seen one before."

The man grinned. "You will. There are trees on this island older than your king. They remember too. But they don't always forgive."

The evening stretched into a humid night. Below deck, the cargo hold filled with the smells of earth and oil. Tomas helped stack the crates in neat rows, noting how Martim checked each one twice, his fingers lingering just a moment too long on a chest covered in goatskin. Its lock gleamed darkly in the lantern light.

When they returned to the deck, the mood was different. Men spoke in hushed tones. Martim's jaw was tight. Vitor stood at the quarterdeck for hours, unmoving.

That night, Diogo whispered, "There are rumours. About something they're not telling us." Tomas leaned in. "What kind of something?"

"I don't know. A shipment. Maybe something hidden. All I know is that Vitor met with a man in a black robe. Didn't even shake his hand."

Tomas didn't reply. But the drumbeat from the island echoed in his mind. It had changed. Slower now. Deeper. Like it was counting down. He dreamt again. This time of fire in the trees. A river turning to ash. And above it all, a faceless shape watching from the canopy, cloaked in vines and flame.

Two days later, they left Sao Tome.

The *Sao Rafael* pulled away with sails full of promise and silence. Whatever they'd taken on board, spices, gold, secrets, it sat heavy in the hold and heavier in the crew's eyes.

Tomas worked without question. He didn't need to ask. He could feel it in the timber. In the way Martim walked. In how Diogo spoke less and less.

He saw it, too, in the old sailor Joan, who now tied charms of shell and bone around the rigging. Protection, he said. From what, he wouldn't say.

The sun was relentless on the third day out, beating the deck like a drum. Crewmen moved slower. Even the gulls seemed too tired to follow.

At dusk, Tomas joined Diogo and Henrique near the stern. They passed a battered flask between them. Rum sweetened with molasses and something herbal.

"You boys ever seen a sea turn black?" Henrique asked, eyes narrowed. Diogo laughed nervously. "No. Should we?"

Henrique pointed west. "Sometimes the ocean remembers too. If we sail through the wrong waters with the wrong cargo, she'll let us know."

One night, as they cut through a still sea under a sky bruised with moonlight, Tomas and Diogo sat aft.

"Do you believe in curses?" Tomas asked.

Diogo didn't laugh. "I believe in people. And people curse everything they touch." They sat in silence after that.

The wind shifted. The stars blinked.

And somewhere in the dark, something followed them.

CHAPTER FIVE

The Shadow Beneath

The wind came from the east now, sharp and constant, as though trying to push them back.

Three days had passed since they left Sao Tome, and the mood aboard the *Sao Rafael* had thinned to whispers and tight, unspeaking jaws. It was as if the sea itself had taken a vow of silence. No one dared voice what gnawed at them, but Tomas felt it. In the weight of the air, heavy like a held breath; in the restless creak of the rigging, which groaned like something alive and uneasy.

Even the sails, taut and white against the pale sky, seemed to strain not from wind but from something unseen, as though resisting a force no one could name. The ocean shimmered with an unnatural calm, a mirror too still, too perfect. It was the kind of quiet that came before a scream.

The ocean had turned a shade darker.

Not black. Not blue. Something in between, like bruised glass left to throb under unseen fingers. It no longer shimmered, it brooded. The light that touched it seemed hesitant, slipping off the surface as if repelled. Even the foam at the prow had changed. It wasn't light or frothy now, but thick, sluggish, almost congealed. It clung to the wood like sap, and when it spilled over the deck, it left behind faint stains. Irregular smudges the colour of old ivory or faded blood.

Tomas crouched once to touch it, and though it felt like seawater, it left a strange tingling on his fingertips, as if the ocean itself were remembering something. Or mourning it. There was no storm. No wind. But the swells moved with the weight of something ancient, as if the ship were passing over a memory the deep had not consented to give up.

That morning, a sailor named Ivo refused to get out of his hammock. When Martim tried to drag him to his feet, Ivo clung to the ropes with white-knuckled fists, eyes wild, breath coming in ragged gasps. He babbled about the ship being watched.

"Eyes in the water," he muttered, voice hoarse and feverish. "Below. Following. Waiting. Like the *Olhos de Sargaco*. You haul them up with the net, and they never blink."

The older sailors crossed themselves. One spat over the rail. Another muttered a prayer to Saint Elmo, tapping his forehead, chest, and the hilt of his knife. No one laughed. They tied Ivo below deck, lashing him gently but firmly to a support beam near the ballast. A clove of garlic was nailed above the hatch, just in case.

Tomas heard him wailing in the night. Long, thin cries that didn't sound quite human, rising and falling with the swell of the sea.

By the fifth day, the crew had stopped singing. Not even Diogo hummed. The sea was too quiet, the skies too calm. A bird landed on the railing once, and every man turned to look. It stayed there for an hour. Watching. Then it flew away toward the west, into the wind.

"It knew something," Henrique muttered. "They always do."

Even Joan's charms seemed dimmer. The shells had dulled, their lustre gone like breath from a mirror. The bones, once smooth and pale, had begun to crack in strange places, hairline fractures like veins of something hidden, splintering under some unseen weight.

One evening, Tomas found Diogo crouched in the hold, unmoving, eyes fixed on the locked goatskin chest nestled between sacks of traded goods. The shadows pressed in around him.

"What is it?" Tomas asked, stepping carefully over coiled rope.

Diogo didn't look away. His voice was barely a whisper. "Something in there's humming. Can't you hear it?"

Tomas leaned closer, placing a hand on the worn leather. Silence. The musty smell of the hold. The groan of the timbers.

"You're tired," he said, though his voice caught.

Diogo nodded slowly, as if agreeing to something he didn't believe. But he didn't move. He stayed there long after Tomas had gone.

That night, Tomas dreamt of the island again. But it wasn't as he remembered. It was burning now. The palms stood blackened and bent like dying men. The trees had mouth; wide, jagged things that chattered without sound. The rivers weren't rivers anymore; they screamed as they flowed uphill, red as rust.

He woke with his hands clenched into fists so tight his nails had bitten his palms. The horizon was empty. A pale smear of dawn stretched above the sea, but it brought no comfort.

On the seventh day, Vitor collapsed at the helm. No wound. No sickness. Just fell, like a marionette whose strings had been quietly snipped. His eyes were open but saw nothing. Martim took the wheel, hands like vices, jaw clenched like iron.

"We keep west," he barked, voice dry as salt. Nobody argued.

Below deck, the air was hotter than it should've been. Thick, swollen, sour. The cacao pods had begun to sweat through their husks, beads of moisture running like tears down their sides. The spices too. One of the sacks had split open, and the scent of cinnamon filled the hold. Not sweet, but sharp and cloying, like a blade slipped beneath the skin.

Henrique whispered to Tomas, his voice a thin thread in the dark. "There are things that shouldn't leave land. Things born of soil and shadow. They belong to roots, to hollows beneath trees, to nights with no moon. Take them to sea."

He looked out at the black water beyond the hull, his eyes haunted. "The sea remembers. And it gets angry."

That night, long after the lanterns had been snuffed out and the men lay restless in their hammocks, someone knocked on the door to the hold.

Three soft taps. Not loud. Not urgent. Almost... polite.

Tomas hesitated, hand hovering near the latch. The wood felt colder than it should. He opened it slowly.

No one was there.

Just the darkness pooling thick between the barrels, the faint scent of wet earth curling up from below. And something else; metallic and sharp. Like iron left too long in blood.

He stood there for a long breath, then shut the door. Bolted it. But the knocking came again.

Three taps. Slower this time. As though whatever it was had all the time in the world.

On the ninth day, the compass began to spin. Slow at first, like a leaf circling a drain, then faster, until it became useless entirely. Martim cursed and hurled it against the mast, where it shattered like brittle glass.

They sailed by the stars after that. But even those betrayed them. They blinked in strange intervals, pulsing in and out of rhythm with the sea. Constellations shifted, just slightly. Enough to make the sky unfamiliar.

One night, Tomas stared up and saw a pattern he had never seen. A curved arc of stars wrapping around a central flare, like a serpent coiled around a tongue of flame.

"Ivo said it had eyes," Diogo whispered from beside him, barely audible over the creak of the ship. "What if it does? What if it's real?"

Tomas wanted to laugh. Say something dismissive. But the words caught like fishbone in his throat. He said nothing.

Later that same night, someone found the goatskin chest in the hold, open.

The contents were untouched. The scrolls, the herbs, the strange bone runes; everything lay as it had. Only the lock was gone. Not broken. Not forced.

Melted.

It lay beside the chest like a dark coin, warped and soft as wax.

The next morning, the wind died completely. The sails hung like dead men, limp and mournful. The sea beneath turned to glass. Still, flawless, and unnatural.

Tomas leaned over the railing, drawn by a sudden stillness deeper than silence. Below, far beneath the keel, something moved. Not a shadow. A shape. Vast. Slow. Too deep to touch. Too clear to miss. It moved in circles, not rising, not retreating.

Diogo appeared beside him, eyes wide. "It's still watching," he whispered.

Tomas didn't answer immediately. He watched the thing below, felt the weight of it. Like the gaze of a world that had been slumbering until their ship crossed some invisible line.

Perhaps this is what his uncle had meant, in half-drunken riddles on Lisbon's docks: that to cross these seas was not merely to travel, but to trespass.

Tomas nodded, finally. But said nothing.Something had awakened. And it wasn't just beneath the water.

It was ahead of them. India.

CHAPTER SIX

When the Wind Changed

They did not see India at first. They felt it.

It came in the air, two weeks after Sao Tome. A change so subtle it was not noticed at once. Not by the eyes, but by the skin, by the breath. The wind shifted, warming gradually until it felt like a hand brushing the face, soft and insistent. There was a sweetness to it now, a perfume threaded through the salt. Distant, elusive, like something remembered from a dream. Scents not born of sea or storm began to drift in. Smoke, perhaps, or crushed leaves, or the ghost of something flowering far away.

The sky changed too. The blue grew deeper, almost velvet by noon, and at dusk, the clouds no longer hung low and grey but floated high and white like veils caught in ceremony. The sun took on a weightier hue, as though it had aged overnight. It's heat familiar, but it's light older, wiser. And at night, the stars sharpened. They burned with a clarity that made Tomas uneasy, brighter and further away, like the heavens themselves were retreating to observe, to witness the threshold being crossed.

The *Sao Rafael* moved slower now. Not out of caution, for the seas were calm. But with a strange deliberateness.

The sails billowed, but the ship seemed to hold its breath. It seemed unwilling to rush towards what was to come. Every creak of wood sounded louder. Every flap of sail more ceremonial. It was not the movement of men chasing a prize. It was the slow, reverent drift of a pilgrim nearing a shrine.

Among the crew, the mood grew sharp-edged and stretched thin. Like rope left too long in salt and sun. Some men grew restless, pacing the decks and fiddling with knots that didn't need tightening. Others turned inward, falling into long silences broken only by the occasional muttered curse or prayer. Mateus, the oldest among the midshipmen, began whispering verses under his breath at every hour. Fragments of Latin hymns no one else understood, crossing himself with such fervour that his fingers trembled.

One of the younger crew, Joao, shaved his head clean with a dull blade, explaining, unasked, that he wanted to meet the new world without the filth of the old clinging to him.

"Fresh skin," he said, tapping his temple. "New eyes." His scalp bled in places, but he didn't flinch.

Diogo, who once filled every silence with laughter or tales, spoke less with each passing day. When he did, it was about food. Not in jest, but with real longing. He spoke of mangoes he'd only heard of in port legends, or coconuts split open on hot stones, or golden fruits with names no tongue aboard could pronounce.

"I want to taste something," he murmured one night, "that's never touched Europe. Something born from different stars."

Even the officers weren't immune. Martim grew quieter. He stood longer at the railing, his usual scowl softened by thought. Joan, the old sailor with charms of bone and shell, stitched new ones every night and hung them in places he never had before. Beneath the tiller, behind the lantern box, even inside his own boots.

And Tomas, Tomas felt it most of all.

There was a hum beneath his skin now, a low, insistent vibration that he couldn't name. It wasn't fear. And it wasn't quite joy. It lived in the hollow space between a thrum of awe, anticipation, and the weight of something about to happen. He caught himself scrubbing the same patch of railing long after it was clean, his hands moving while his mind wandered. He woke before the bell, before the gulls, before the light even cracked the sky.

His dreams had changed too. The island of fire was gone. In its place came visions that pulsed with colour. Shifting, impossible colours that seemed to breathe and ripple like silk underwater. He dreamt of cities not built, but grown. Of towers that curved like petals and streets lined with lamps that flickered without flame. Rivers glowed with inner light, and trees whispered in voices older than wind. And always, there were eyes. Not watching in judgment, but simply watching. Still. Patient. As if they had been waiting for him since long before he was born. The sea changed colour again.

It turned the green of oxidised bronze. Not sickly, but deep. Alive. Flying fish skimmed the waves, flashing silver in the sun. Unfamiliar flocks of birds passed overhead. There was no land yet. But the world had begun to speak differently.

Vasco da Gama stood at the prow on the twenty-fourth day, unmoving.

He hadn't spoken to the crew in days. His meals were brought to his quarters. His boots clicked across the deck at dawn and again before dusk. Otherwise, he was still. Watching. Calculating.

That morning, he watched the sun rise with a stillness that unnerved even Martim.

Tomas saw him from afar. Not a grand figure. Not the stuff of legend. Just a man in a cloak too thin for the wind, with a face carved by salt and obsession.

But there was something in his posture. Something in the way he stared at the horizon like he'd known it all his life.

"This is what he's lived for," Diogo whispered. "It's like he's seeing a ghost that finally agreed to appear."

No one dared disturb him. Even Martim, who grumbled orders under his breath and snapped at younger sailors, lowered his voice when Da Gama passed. The captain had grown leaner on the voyage, but not weaker. His silence had gravity. And to Tomas, he seemed less a man now and more a monument. One that knew it would be remembered.

There were whispers about the chest again.

The lock hadn't been replaced. It sat inside the captain's quarters now, under guard. Tomas passed the door once at night and heard something. A faint sound, like paper rustling, or a breath drawn inward. The guard at the door refused to meet his eye.

They all knew it was meant for India. They didn't know what it was.

Henrique, who usually laughed off superstition, began to leave offerings in the hold. Bits of food, a coin, a carving of a fish he'd whittled from driftwood. He didn't explain. No one asked.

"It needs to be fed," he muttered once.

On the twenty-seventh day, the lookout called: "Land Ahoy!"

Chaos followed. Cheers. Shouts. Some men wept. Others dropped to their knees. A sailor carved a small cross into the deck with his knife.

It was a dark line on the horizon, low and long, like the back of something ancient sleeping in the sea.

Da Gama didn't cheer. He didn't smile.

He simply exhaled. One long breath. Then turned away.

That night, there was no sleep.

The sails were trimmed. The men scrubbed their boots. Ropes were re-coiled. Salt stains were rubbed out of coats. Everything had to look right. There were arguments about who would step ashore first. Bets placed. Silent prayers whispered over coins and charms.

Tomas stood on the deck and watched the outline of India grow teeth. Palms, cliffs, the skeletal tips of distant towers.

He thought of Lisbon.

The dark streets. The stench of boiling leather. The narrow sky. And now this.

His pulse quickened. It wasn't only that the voyage had brought them to land. It was that the land itself seemed to lean toward them, as though it had expected them. As though it had been watching them arrive.

A hush fell over the ship, unspoken but felt. The waves lapped softer. The wind slowed. Even the gulls kept their distance.

The next morning, India rose from the mist.

It did not burst into view like a revelation. It unfolded, slow, solemn, inevitable. As though it had always been there, waiting just beyond the reach of their world. It was not golden. It was not bright.

It was dense. Green. Rooted. As if the land had grown from the bones of old gods, shaped not by hands but by memory and myth. It stretched wide across the horizon, quiet and still, but brimming with presence. The kind of presence that made even the wind hesitate.

The coast was lined with trees taller than sails, their canopies braided into a living wall that swayed with its own breath. Vines hung like veils from ancient boughs. Flashes of colour, bright birds, blooming flowers, darted and shimmered like secrets refusing to be caught. The sand below was not white, but red, like powdered coral or crushed brick, glowing softly in the morning light.

Birds with tails, soared above the treetops. Curling and diving in arcs that seemed choreographed. Their cries echoed across the water, unlike anything the crew had heard before. In the distance, thin plumes of smoke curled gently into the sky from villages unseen. Rising like prayers from the jungle's hidden heart.

And the air, Tomas would remember it forever.

It smelled of clove and woodsmoke, yes, but layered within that was something deeper. The scent of fruit so ripe, it bordered on ferment. Of bark and resin, of earth after a long rain. Sweetness without sugar. Spice without fire. It was the smell of a place that had never been conquered. Never been named.

For a long moment, no one aboard spoke. They stood along the rail in stillness, hats in hand, as if they had arrived not at a destination, but at the edge of a sacred truth. Something older than language. Something vast and alive.

They dropped anchor in a calm bay. Small boats approached, painted, swift, full of men in turbans and loose cottons. They bore no weapons. Only curiosity.

Diogo gripped Tomas's shoulder. "We've found it!" he exclaimed with barely concealed excitement. "No," Tomas whispered. "We're about to."

He couldn't tear his eyes away. The boats were coming faster now, paddles dipping like clockwork. Voices drifted across the water. Unfamiliar syllables, rising and falling like music. Some of the younger sailors backed away from the rail. Others leaned forward, eyes wide.

Tomas stayed still. He wanted to memorise the moment. The line where sea met land. The place where maps ended and myth began.

Later, in the captain's quarters, the goatskin chest was opened.

Only three men were present: Vasco da Gama, Martim, and the first translator; an educated Moor taken aboard at Mozambique, whose eyes had grown more guarded the closer they sailed to the Indian coast.

The chest opened with a soft groan, the hinges reluctant, the air inside heavy with age. For a few seconds, there was silence. Not awe. Not reverence. Something stranger. Like recognition.

What they saw inside, no one else knew. But those who passed by the quarters afterward claimed they smelled something sharp and unfamiliar. Sandalwood, yes, but also ink, copper, and a strange floral note that lingered even after the door shut.

The translator had gone pale.

Later that day, Da Gama's orders changed. He would meet the local ruler himself.

And the chest, sealed again, its lock replaced with a fresh clasp bound in iron and wax, would go with him.

Some whispered that it held gifts fit for a king: fine silks, gold thread, relics from Jerusalem. Others claimed it was something older. A map. A letter. A piece of knowledge meant not to impress, but to command. Tomas never saw it again.

But he dreamed that night of parchment that burned without flame, of a script he could not read glowing under his skin. And of eyes, not watching him, but waiting. It was also accompanied by some sort of odour. Not spice. Not salt. Something ancient. Something carved from smoke and belief. It clung to the wood. It whispered in the grain. And in his bones, Tomas felt the world shift.

India had not just been found. It had been stirred.

CHAPTER SEVEN

The Edge of the Known World

Calicut, 1498

The smell came first.

Long before land was visible. Before even the crow's cries had shifted and the gulls circled lower in hopeful arcs, the scent reached them. A warm, perfumed breath from the East: brine mingled with cardamom, sandalwood, strange unknown flowers, and woodsmoke. It was faint at first, like a memory unspooling through the air, but it deepened with every gust of wind that touched the sails.

Da Gama stood at the prow, his knuckles white on the rail, eyes rimmed red not from the salt spray but from something deeper. He had stopped blinking, it seemed, unwilling to let the world shift even a degree from what it now offered: the possibility of destiny fulfilled.

Behind him, the men stirred. The deck creaked beneath their boots. After weeks of rot and thirst, of bitter waters and prayers shouted into empty skies, the crew had become hushed, reverent. They, too, smelled it now. Even the cynics, the mutterers, the hard-knuckled Galicians who scoffed at myth, fell quiet.

It was real.

India.

Tomas stood beside the mainmast, the sun glinting off his shaved scalp. He held the chest now not with fear, but purpose. Its edges were frayed from the voyage, and its lock had turned greenish with sea air, but whatever rested inside had not spoken again. Not aloud. Yet Tomas had begun to feel it in his dreams. Small, flickering pulses like moths inside a lantern. Something old, something waiting.

Da Gama turned to the helmsman.

"Hold course. Due east. Let her feel the coast before she sees it."

The helmsman nodded, saying nothing. The sea had changed, its blue darkening with depth, with life. Flying fish zipped ahead, and silver fins crested in the wake. This was not the Atlantic's blankness. This was a warm, inhabited ocean. As if it had been waiting for them.

At midday, land appeared.

A brown-green smudge across the horizon, growing clearer with every breath. Trees first. Palm and coconut, dense with birds. Then, as if the sea pulled back a curtain, the sprawl of Calicut: a city of carved stone and red-tiled roofs, bazaars stacked like honeycombs. Temples rising above thatched huts, all shimmering under the molten haze of the Malabar sun.

Da Gama's lips parted, but he said nothing.

In his mind, he saw the map of the world, the great parchment he'd stared at since his youth in Sines. The place where the ink thinned. Where cartographers drew sea monsters and winds with wings, marking their ignorance with flourish. He had once traced a finger along that edge and whispered, *"Here. Here is where I'll go."*

And now, he was *here.*

A great exhale left him, the first full breath in months. He fell to his knees.

The crew, watching, followed without command. One by one, they sank to the deck, heads bowed. Even the surly ones, even Joao with his torn leg and the whispering Galician boy. Even Tomas, chest beside him, lips moving in a silent prayer.

Da Gama looked up at the sky, where the sails hung still.

"Obrigado," he murmured. "For the winds. For the stars. For the bones we buried along the way. And for this moment, which is more than a man deserves."

He remembered his brother Paulo, buried beneath the African sands. Remembered the fever dreams, the mutiny at Mombasa, the hollow-eyed translator they had bartered from a Swahili dhow. He remembered hunger like a wound, and the way hope had thinned to a thread he'd wrapped around his heart so tightly it nearly stopped beating.

And yet, here he was.

They made landfall near dusk.

A canoe came first, carved from blackened teak, rowed by four men in crisp white dhotis. Their skin gleamed like copper, and they bore garlands of jasmine around their necks. At the helm sat a man with eyes like polished onyx and a turban of gold-threaded red.

He did not speak Portuguese, but bowed deeply. The gesture was one of welcome, not submission.

Da Gama, in return, touched hand to heart and inclined his head. He let Pedro Alvares, their Moorish interpreter, speak the formalities.

Words flowed back and forth like silk: Who are you? Where from? Why here?

When the stranger learned they had come from the West to trade, to seek pepper, ivory, spices, the man nodded, unsurprised. Da Gama wondered how many had come before him? Arabs, Chinese, even the Venetians in disguise.

Yet something in the man's smile said: *You are different. You've come through fire. You've come to stay.*

"Tomorrow," the interpreter said, turning to Da Gama, "we are summoned to the Zamorin's court. He will receive you."

Da Gama nodded slowly.

Tomas touched the chest. "Should we bring it?" Da Gama looked at it for a long time.

Not yet.

That night, they anchored in the harbour of Calicut.

Torches burned along the piers, casting long shadows on water. The scent of saffron rice, tamarind, and roasted meats drifted across the surf. Music, unlike any they had heard, echoed. Pipes and bells, with a kind of rhythm that felt circular, eternal.

The crew remained mostly aboard, save for the emissaries. They huddled together, not from fear, but awe. They spoke little. What words were there?

Tomas sat beside the chest on the upper deck, staring at the lights. He turned as Da Gama approached.

"She's beautiful," Tomas said, gesturing toward the city. "Yes."

"Do you think they'll welcome us?" Da Gama didn't answer at first.

"I think," he said finally, "that we're not the first to dream of this shore. But dreams leave marks. And ours, he looked toward the city, then down at the chest, might cut deeper than the rest."

Tomas hesitated. "Sometimes, I think I hear her. Not with ears. Like a whisper under my ribs." "Her?"

"The one inside. Whatever was sealed in this chest. It's not an object. It's not gold. It's old. Older than Portugal, older than this land. Sometimes I think it knows we're here."

Da Gama looked down at the ornate carvings. Runes older than Latin curled along its sides. Some from the Nile, some from Indian scripts he did not recognise.

He'd found it buried beneath an old monastery in Madeira. Hidden inside a wall, sealed in wax and sandalwood, marked only with the phrase: *"For the East, and no other."*

He had brought it because something told him to. Not orders. Not greed. But intuition. "Tomas," he said softly, "you're to come with me tomorrow. Into the city."

"And the chest?"

"No. It stays. For now."

At dawn, the sky burned rose-gold. Monkeys chattered from coconut palms. A breeze, thick with life, stirred the Portuguese sails like a benediction.

Da Gama dressed in his finest coat of dark velvet with gold trim. It featured the royal crest of Portugal emblazoned on the breast. Around his neck, hung a simple chain. He looked less like a conqueror, more like a penitent priest walking into a shrine.

Tomas walked beside him, quieter than usual.

The canoe bore them across the harbour, its hull slicing through waters that shimmered like hammered brass under the morning sun. The scent of the sea gave way, slowly, to something richer.

Cinnamon, clove, sandalwood, and the faintest trace of burning ghee. The air was thick with promise, heady with unfamiliar life. As they drew closer to the shore, the sounds of India rose to greet them. Not as a cacophony, but as a kind of symphony: conch shells, temple bells, distant drumming, and the high call of a muezzin echoing from somewhere unseen.

A crowd had gathered along the sandbanks. Not angry, not hostile. Curious. Eyes of every shade and shape tracked the foreigners in the boat. Children with skin like polished bronze ran barefoot along the dunes, laughing, fearless. Some of them pointed at Tomas and mimicked his strange hat; one girl threw him a flower. Women leaned from latticed balconies, their arms adorned with bangles that caught the light, their saris flowing in ripples of emerald, crimson, and turmeric-yellow. It was as though a living painting had spilled out onto the streets to welcome them.

The air hummed with a kind of expectant tension. Something more ancient. Something Da Gama could not name, but could feel down to the marrow. The hairs on his arms stood erect, stirred by that deep, eternal current. He felt it then; not as a captain, not even as a man of the Crown, but as a soul adrift on the edge of a myth he had longed to enter all his life.

At the gates of the city, under an arch of rose-hued stone chiseled with patterns like prayers, guards in jewelled turbans stepped aside in solemn choreography. Bronze anklets jingled as they moved. And then, like the opening of a spellbound book, the streets of Calicut unfolded before them, each page richer than the last.

Spice merchants stood beside heaped pyramids of cardamom and pepper, saffron folded in cloth like fire. Glass-blowers spun molten light into baubles and bangles as bright as the sky at dawn. Dancers with *kohled* eyes and anklets of silver performed in slow, sacred rhythm near shrines garlanded with jasmine. Scribes dipped peacock-feather pens into inkwells of indigo and gold, their fingers stained with stories.

Languages twisted together in the warm breeze; Arabic, Tamil, Sanskrit, Kannada, and some tongues Da Gama could not even name. They flowed like a river of voices, uncontainable, multilingual, ancient and alive. Tomas turned in every direction, his mouth half-open in astonishment, his sketchbook forgotten in his satchel.

And above it all, majestic and serene, the palace of the Zamorin rose on the crest of the city, carved from stone the colour of sun-baked honey. Its spires pierced the sky like the domes of old epics; balconies jutted like prows of ships. Fluttering banners bore symbols Tomas could not decipher.

Serpents, elephants, stars. But they pulsed with meaning all the same. Behind its golden doors, a ruler waited. But it was India itself that had already received them, with the boundless grace of something older than kingdoms.

Inside, the throne room was a vault of shadows and incense. The Zamorin sat on a platform of rosewood, garlanded, silent. His gaze was not hostile. But neither was it warm.

He was a man carved from stillness, neither young nor old, but ageless in the way of stone idols. His skin was dark and lustrous, his bare chest marked with sandalwood paste in the sacred design of a rising sun. Around his neck hung a garland of *rudraksha* and jasmine, incongruous yet regal. His eyes were sharp, fathomless pools under heavy lids, watching not just what was before him but what lay beneath it. A golden turban wrapped tightly around his head shimmered with embedded rubies, and from his ears hung elongated ornaments shaped like serpents swallowing their own tails.

He did not speak, but his silence weighed more than any speech. His fingers, long and elegant, rested lightly on the armrests of the throne. They were long and adorned with rings of greenstone and ivory. A thin smile played at the corners of his lips, but it was unreadable, like a script lost to time.

The chamber breathed like a temple. Dark, fragrant, slow. Shafts of sunlight filtered in through carved stone latticework high above, laying intricate patterns on the floor like scattered blessings or ancient warnings. Every surface seemed touched by time: the stone tiles beneath their feet bore the soft polish of a thousand footfalls; the rosewood throne gleamed with oil and age; incense curled in silent plumes from copper censers shaped like lotuses and lions.

Attendants stood along the periphery in complete stillness, their dhotis spotless, their faces expressionless. Musicians with *veenas* and mridangams sat poised but unsummoned, as if the room itself waited to exhale. Peacocks embroidered in gold-thread tapestries seemed to turn their eyes ever so slightly toward the foreigners. A great bronze lamp hung from the vaulted ceiling, unlit, but pregnant with the suggestion of ritual.

Da Gama, a man seasoned in storms and courts alike, found himself oddly off-balance. He had stood before kings in Lisbon, debated princes in Morocco, even spoken through interpreters to tribal chieftains along the African coast. But never had silence held such dominion. Never had a court made such a show of restraint, of power cloaked not in spectacle but in patience. It was a performance in which he was both audience and unwitting actor.

Tomas, standing just behind Da Gama, felt it too. that weight of presence, like standing in the court of Solomon. He would later struggle to recall the precise features of the Zamorin's face, but never the sensation. It was as if he had looked into a mirror that did not show his own reflection, but the vast span of something eternal.

Tomas shifted his weight and immediately regretted it. The faint squeak of his leather sole on polished stone seemed to echo through the room like an offence. No one turned. But he could feel dozens of gazes. Hidden behind lattice screens or perched in gallery balconies. Watching. Weighing.

A small procession emerged from a side corridor. Priests, or perhaps ministers, clad in ochre robes and bearing scrolls, betel leaves, and golden salvers. They moved with the deliberation of clockwork, placing each item at the base of the platform before retreating wordlessly into the incense-thick gloom. One of them knelt and whispered something into the Zamorin's ear. The ruler did not nod. He did not blink. His hand moved just a fraction, two fingers raised like a whisper of wind.

And then, finally, a voice.

Not the Zamorin's. But that of a man who stepped forward from the shadows on the right. A figure draped in white silk, with a face as composed as an ivory mask and eyes sharp as flint.

"The *Samoothiri* will now hear your words," the man said, his Portuguese tinged with the softness of Malayalam. "Speak, Vasco da Gama, emissary of the Western seas."

The words rang out with ceremonial weight. Tomas instinctively bowed his head. Da Gama, steadying his breath, stepped forward. His journey had ended here. Or perhaps it had only just begun. He looked into the Zamorin's eyes. And in that glance, across oceans, across centuries of trade and myth and ambition, something passed between them.

Not friendship. But recognition.

Later, as they returned to the ship, Tomas asked: "Do you think he believed you?" "No," Da Gama said. "But

I think he believed I believe. And is that enough?" "For now".

That night, Da Gama stood alone at the prow again, wind in his hair, the lights of Calicut behind him like a dream given form. He touched the rail, then the pendant at his throat. A small wooden carving his mother had given him. He had not worn it in months. Now it seemed to hum.

He looked back toward the captain's quarters, where the chest rested. There was no sound. No light. And yet, he felt it. Aware, watching, waiting.

He spoke aloud, not knowing why: "We've arrived."

And for the first time since Madeira, a voice whispered inside his mind.

Yes.

And it begins again.

The Language of Belief

The air on deck was salt-laced and restless. Lanterns swung on rigging lines like slow metronomes of unease. Tomas stood near the stern, quill in hand, parchment weighted with brass coins to keep the wind from stealing it. The horizon was dark now, Calicut reduced to a scatter of distant lamps, yet the encounter still pulsed in his mind—too vivid, too strange to settle.

He turned as footsteps approached. Diogo, lean and sun-cured, with a strip of cloth around his brow, came to stand beside him. "You look like a man who's seen a ghost."

"I've seen something older," Tomas murmured, eyes not leaving the sea. "Do you have a moment? I think you should know what was said in the court."

Diogo leaned against the rail. "I'm listening." And so Tomas told it.

He described the throne room again, the way it felt like being swallowed by a legend. He described the silence that hung before speech like a blade waiting to fall. And then, carefully, he repeated the words Da Gama had offered to the Zamorin.

Not trade. Not power. Not conquest. But destiny.

Da Gama had spoken, through the interpreter, of a prophecy. An old Western belief that the sea route to India would unlock the world's balance. That it would not only unite riches but unravel divine threads long severed. That he, Vasco da Gama, was not merely a servant of the Portuguese crown, but anointed—by circumstance or fate—as the one to fulfil this ancient crossing. The navigator who closed the loop between East and West.

Some in the court had scoffed. Others, Tomas noticed, had not. They had listened, still as stone. A few exchanged glances, subtle and unreadable. There had been a moment when even the Zamorin's half-lidded eyes had seemed to stir. Not with belief, but with interest.

"That was his meaning," Tomas said at last, his voice low, shaped by the weight of what had passed. "He doubts the Zamorin took his words for truth. But he saw something else in him. Not deception. Not performance. But conviction."

Diogo remained silent for a moment too long, the wind tugging gently at his hair. Then, without looking at Tomas, he asked, "And you? Do you believe?"

Tomas's fingers tightened around the rail. "Belief," he said slowly, "is the most dangerous thing a man can carry. It doesn't have to be right. It only needs to be seen. And once seen, whether by friend or foe, it becomes real."

By morning, the city felt colder.

Word had spread among the local merchants that Da Gama's gifts; tapestries, coral, silver trinkets, had not impressed. That the Zamorin had offered audience, but not alliance. Some said the Portuguese had no true power, only elaborate manners and tall stories. Others whispered of things left unspoken in the court. The mention of stars, of destiny, of East meeting West not in trade, but in time.

The sailors picked up on the mood, and soon unease took root aboard the fleet. Joao, one of the younger men, muttered of cursed ports and charmed idols. Another swore they'd been watched by shadowy figures on the docks. Tomas tried to calm them, but he too had sensed something—an undercurrent, elusive and ancient, as if Calicut itself were studying them through veiled eyes.

That evening, Da Gama summoned his closest officers. The captain's quarters were lit with a single lantern and the half-light of dusk. The astrolabe from the chest lay on the table before them, the strange inscription catching the flame with each motion of the ship.

"I've sent word requesting another audience," Da Gama said. "But I expect silence. We are being measured now—not for our worth, but our endurance."

"Then what do we do?" Diogo asked.

"We wait. We listen. And we learn." Da Gama tapped the chest. "This was given to us for a reason. But it is not a gift. It is a test."

"What sort of test?" Tomas asked.

"That's what we must find out."

Over the next three days, a strange rhythm settled over the fleet.

Tomas spent his hours studying the chest, sketching its contours and trying to match the unfamiliar constellations with what he knew of the southern skies. Da Gama became more withdrawn, walking the decks at dawn and dusk, murmuring to himself. Diogo handled the men, who grew more anxious with each day that passed without invitation or hostility.

It was two nights later that a summons arrived. Unexpected and unscripted.A Brahmin emissary, flanked by silent guards, came aboard with a simple message: "Come to the temple. Alone."

Da Gama insisted on taking Tomas.

The streets at night were different. Less spectacle, more shadow. Dogs barked from alleyways. Firelight flickered from shrines where idols stood half-bathed in marigolds and blood. The temple was not large, but it was old. Older, perhaps, than Lisbon itself.

Inside, a mural stretched across the domed ceiling: a churning ocean, a snake coiled around a mountain, gods and demons pulling against each other. *Samudra Manthan*, the interpreter whispered. The churning of the ocean of milk. The search for *Amrita*. Immortality.

They were led to a courtyard. There, an old man waited, dressed in white, a single strand of rudraksha around his neck. He did not speak immediately. When he did, it was in slow, deliberate Portuguese.

"You speak of prophecy," he said. "But India has her own."

Da Gama inclined his head. "I do not claim to rewrite yours. Only to see if ours and yours are not strangers."

The old man studied him. "Then listen."

And he spoke of rivers, and wheels of time, and foreign kings who would one day arrive bearing fire and silence. Some to build, some to consume. He spoke of a land that never forgot, only waited.

When the moon reached its zenith, he handed Da Gama a single object: a small, obsidian disc etched with a script none of them could read. "This belongs to your chest," the old man said. "It was never ours. But we were told you would come."

Back aboard the ship, under a sky bruised with stars, Tomas placed the disc into the chest's curved slot.

With a sound like breath escaping, the lock turned. The lid creaked open.

And inside, wrapped in layers of linen and time, lay an astrolabe.

But not like any they had ever seen. It was made of blackened brass, its rim etched with constellations unfamiliar to European skies. The central plate bore both Western numerals and symbols from Indian *siddhantic* astronomy. And around its edge, in faded gold, was a single inscription. Half in Latin, half in Sanskrit.

Da Gama read it aloud.

"To chart the stars is not to escape fate, but to understand its orbit."

He stared down at it, his breath catching in his throat. "This," he whispered, "is not a tool for sailors." "No," Tomas said. "It's a key."

And then, one morning, as the tide shifted beneath a sunless sky, a messenger arrived again.

This time, the message was not from the Zamorin. It was from one of his rivals. A lesser noble, a spice merchant turned court advisor, who offered what the Zamorin would not: a private meeting. No interpreters. No formalities.

Da Gama agreed.

The house was outside the city's walls, on a rise above the backwaters. It smelled of sandalwood and camphor, with low ceilings and carved panels depicting celestial scenes. The noble, a Rajan Nair, was young, sharp-eyed, and dressed plainly. He welcomed them with betel leaves and a question.

"Why did you come really?" he asked in fluent Portuguese. "Not the king's version. Yours."

Da Gama did not lie. "I came for the sea route. For the riches of the Indies. For the edge Portugal needs."

Nair smiled faintly. "That's a good answer. But not the full one."

Da Gama met his gaze. "I came because I had to. I came because there is something in me that believes this is where the future begins."

The noble looked at him a long time, then nodded. "There are old texts here, Palm-leaf manuscripts. They speak of visitors from across the sea who would come not for war, but for answers. They would carry old knowledge dressed as new. You speak as one of them."

He motioned to a servant, who brought in a cloth-wrapped bundle. When opened, it revealed a second disk. It looked similar to the one from the temple, but bearing lunar markings.

"Yours?" Da Gama asked.

"No. It was found in a shipwreck years ago. But it matches the design of what your man carries. If you are here for belief, then take this. But beware. Belief is not always welcomed. Especially when it comes ashore dressed as ambition."

That night, the second disc unlocked a compartment within the astrolabe itself. It revealed a series of inner dials that shifted not only by stars, but by *calendar*. The device was a map of time as much as space.

Tomas stared at it, wonderstruck. "It tells *when* as well as where," he whispered. "Like some... celestial oracle."

Da Gama traced the curve with his finger. "Then we must learn to read it. Before others do."

He turned to the crew. "This journey was never only about trade. That was the excuse. This knowledge, this mystery—it's the heart. And now we are part of it."

The next day dawned cloudless and sharp-edged. The crew was restless. Supplies were running low, and the interactions with the locals were growing thinner, cooler. There were whispers among the sailors that the court had no intention of allowing trade, at least not freely. That the Hindu merchants of Calicut, powerful and entrenched, saw them not as allies but as intruders.

In the privacy of the captain's quarters, Da Gama poured over scrolls and charts. Tomas sat nearby, the mystery chest still at his feet. He had taken to sleeping near it now, as if proximity might coax its secrets forth. The lock, intricate and foreign, remained untouched.

"We are not the first to come bearing gifts," Da Gama muttered. "But we may be the first to come bearing belief."

He rose and paced. "They expected gold. Incense. Tribute. But we gave them myth. That was the mistake. Or maybe it was the offering they didn't know how to accept."

Tomas looked up. "What if belief is not enough?" "Then we will find what is."

The Fabled Land

The next day broke with a thick haze rising from the backwaters, golden and ghostlike in the morning sun. Da Gama remained aboard the ship, consulting charts and staring endlessly at the astrolabe. As if its spinning dials might whisper the next step in a language only he could one day learn. But Tomas, restless with wonder, asked for leave to go ashore.

It was granted, but with a cautious nod. "Take two men. Stay near the markets." Tomas did not listen to the last part.

He passed through the same city gates as before, but without the grandeur of that first arrival. No procession this time. Just foot traffic and ox-carts, the clatter of brass, the rustle of silks, and the slow, rhythmic chants of traders calling out their wares. And yet the magic was stronger now, because this was no staged welcome. This was India as it lived, breathed, and dreamed.

The streets were a living mural.

Women in saris of every shade; saffron, peacock blue, pomegranate red, moved with grace, their anklets ringing like wind chimes. Men with turbans, bare-chested and broad-shouldered, carried trays of spices or balanced baskets of betel leaves on their heads. Hawkers sold marinated jackfruit and sweetened coconut milk in terracotta cups. A boy painted with ash offered jasmine garlands in exchange for coins, reciting blessings in a voice far too solemn for his age.

Tomas stopped before a temple courtyard where dancers twirled in a whorl of gold and white, their feet striking the stone with divine percussion. A drumbeat rose behind them and a flute wept above it like a whisper on fire.

He had no words to describe what he felt. Awe seemed too small a term.

He bought a piece of banana-leaf-wrapped halwa from a street vendor and let it melt on his tongue, sweet and earthy with the taste of ghee and roasted flour. He saw glass bangles stacked like rainbows, watched a silversmith etch tiny elephants into the side of a pendant. He passed under arches of flowering vines where parrots flitted above like flying gems, green and crimson.

At one stall, he paused to inspect a small statue of Ganesha carved from sandalwood. The merchant grinned. "For luck," he said in Arabic-accented Portuguese. "You are far from home."

Tomas nodded. "And yet... I don't feel far."

The merchant gave him the statue anyway, refusing payment. "Then perhaps, in some other life, you were not."

Back at the docks, other members of the crew were finding their own glimpses of wonder.

Miguel had struck up a trade for a bolt of handwoven cotton dyed indigo so rich it seemed to drink the sun. Joao claimed he'd seen a sacred cow meander through a royal garden and not be stopped. Even dour Baltasar returned with stories of monkeys trained to collect coins and return with ripe mangoes.

Yet for all the marvels, they were being watched.

Tomas noticed it first. An old man lingering too long in the shade of a spice stall. A pair of youths dressed as servants who followed them across three alleys. A flicker of gold in an upper window. Too quick to catch, too deliberate to ignore.

Calicut was open, but not unguarded.

And there were factions, Tomas realised. Whispers that the Zamorin's court was divided. Softly at first, like wind through a reed curtain. Then louder, more insistent, each voice tinted with a different hue of ambition.

Some in the court, especially the younger nobles and merchants tied to the Arab trade, looked upon the Portuguese with cautious intrigue. Foreigners, yes, but perhaps useful ones. They saw the glint of opportunity in their exotic weapons, in the steel of their ships, in the wealth promised from the West. They spoke of alliances, of new sea routes that might enrich Calicut even further, and whispered that the Portuguese arrival had been foretold not as a calamity, but as a correction. They called it destiny.

But others; older lords, Brahmin advisors, and guardians of the old temples, saw rot in this glittering arrival. They called the newcomers *Varanga Yavanas*, 'wandering Greeks, a term for all manner of outsiders' and feared what would follow in their wake. They had seen it before: traders who became rulers, guests who became masters. They spoke in hushed tones of Malabar's long memory and warned the Zamorin that smiles on foreign lips often hid swords.

Even within the priestly caste, there was division. The temple astrologers were said to have cast elaborate charts the night before the Portuguese landed. Stars had danced strangely in the sky, they claimed, constellations veering off course. One senior *jyotishi* proclaimed that *Rahu*, the devourer of the moon, had risen too soon, and in the wrong house. An omen of shadow cloaked in light.

Foreign storms dressed as kings, he warned. Lions that walked like lambs. And still others within the palace walls had their own secrets.

There was a chamberlain with a tattoo of a crescent moon behind his ear, who sent coded messages on palm-leaf scrolls hidden in sandalwood shipments. A courtesan who listened from behind ivory screens, feeding knowledge to a Tamil prince exiled two provinces north. A scribe who kept two ledgers. One for the court, and one for a group of Arab traders who paid handsomely to stay a step ahead of any shifting winds.

The Zamorin himself was a man caught in the centre of this widening gyre. On his left, his chief minister. A sharp-eyed, soft-spoken man who argued for caution, for diplomacy, for seeing where this road might lead. On his right, the palace commander. A rigid, war-scarred veteran, who insisted the newcomers be sent away, or else contained. Neither agreed. Both smiled too much.

And in the shadows behind them, the queen mother whispered to the Zamorin with the weight of generations in her voice. They must not be trusted, she said. Those who speak of gold rarely come for peace.

By late afternoon, Tomas found himself back near the palace gates, where Brahmin priests passed in flowing saffron robes, their voices trailing mantras that shimmered in the heated air like smoke. The scent of sandalwood lingered on his skin, and somewhere beyond the high walls, temple bells chimed in slow, rhythmic patterns. More breath than sound.

He sat on the carved rim of a step well shaded by a flowering neem tree, watching the city fold itself into the long shadows of evening. The day's light had softened, pouring gold over the tiled courtyards and the pale stone walls. Calicut was not one city, he thought, but many. Stacked atop each other like veils: market and shrine, palace and slum, truth and theatre.

Near the palace lawn, a group of children played at war and peace. They were barefoot and joyous, stick swords clashing in imagined battles, their little bodies darting across flagstones in complicated allegiances. One wore a brass bowl for a crown, declaring himself emperor of lands he likely couldn't name. Another hoisted a dry palm frond like a banner, shouting something with fierce conviction. The words were lost on Tomas, but the meaning was not.

One of them; a younger boy, perhaps seven or eight, wandered away from the game and stopped near the step well. He looked at Tomas, wide-eyed and open-faced, studying him with all the unfiltered curiosity children are born with. He said something in Malayalam, the cadence musical, the question evident in his tilted head.

Tomas smiled, lifted a hand in greeting. "I don't understand," he said softly, knowing the boy wouldn't understand that either.

The child repeated himself, then pointed toward the ships in the harbour, then back at Tomas. His meaning, like his voice, was simple: *Who are you?*

Tomas mimed a little ship with his hands, then pointed out to sea. He touched his own chest, and then touched his heart, a quiet gesture. The boy considered him a moment longer, then broke into a smile so pure it almost startled Tomas. Without another word, he plucked a red hibiscus from the edge of the step well and handed it to him, nodding solemnly, as if offering a sword.

Tomas accepted the flower, touched his fingers to his brow in thanks.

Then the boy was gone, racing back to his army of laughing kings and warring princes. Tomas remained where he sat, the hibiscus in his palm. Its petals bled crimson against the roughness of his skin. It was only a child's gift, but it felt like something more. A peace offering in a language older than words.

That evening, Tomas returned to the ship with arms full of nothing. No spices, no silks, no scrolls of trade. But his eyes held more light than when he'd left. Dust still clung to his boots, and the scent of incense and sweet tamarind lingered faintly on his clothes.

He found Da Gama still on deck, staring westward, the sea darkening into ink behind him. A map lay spread before him, pinned at the corners with rusted nails and coral-stained stones. Beside it, the astrolabe lay half-forgotten, glinting under the rising stars.

"There's a world here," Tomas said quietly, voice still touched with wonder. "More than we guessed. More than we can name."

"I know," Da Gama said, without turning. "And it's not ours to take."

"No," Da Gama replied. He touched the edge of the map, tracing a line down the Malabar coast. "But it is ours to understand. To chart with care. And perhaps to shape a bridge between what we carry and what we've found."

He looked down at the astrolabe, which now seemed almost foreign itself. Its etched moons and jagged calibrations no longer pointing to the heavens above, but to forces stranger and more grounded. "We've seen the maps," he said. "Now we must read the land. Not with greed. With clarity. There are more powers at play here than trade alone. The Zamorin watches. So do his priests. And others beyond the court whisper of us in languages we don't yet know how to listen to."

He paused. "The crew speaks of offers made in shadow. Of guides with double tongues. Of merchants who weigh coin with prophecy."

Tomas frowned slightly. "And yet, the people. They live as if eternity is woven into each hour. I saw children rule kingdoms drawn in dust. And a boy who gave me a flower like a treaty."

Da Gama nodded, his eyes lifting toward the temple skyline. "The soul of this land runs deep. We must decide how far we dare wade."

Above them, the stars blinked awake, veiled in the breath of monsoon winds still far to the south. In the east, over the temple domes and minarets, the moon rose. Half full, silver, and watching. Its light touched the water and turned it to quicksilver.

Somewhere in the city, a bell rang. Low, sonorous, eternal. It did not mark time. It marked a turning.

A beginning.

CHAPTER TEN

The Boy Who Knew the Wind

The days in Calicut had taken on the cadence of tides. Slow at first, and then sudden, sweeping, full of undercurrents. Da Gama spent his hours navigating a different kind of ocean now. One of silences and syllables, of glances passed like scrolls in courtly halls. The Zamorin had not spoken to him since their first meeting, but his court had grown warmer, and more dangerous.

There were gifts now. Bracelets of coral, jars of fragrant sandal oil, folded cloth finer than wind. But gifts, Da Gama knew, were never just gifts. They were chess moves. And he had yet to determine the shape of the game. He began keeping notes by candlelight, journaling in margins: Who speaks for the Zamorin? What is the power of the temple vs. the court? What do they seek from us, if not our gold?

Some answers lay within reach. Others were buried, like salt beneath the sea.

Tomas, meanwhile, drifted where he pleased. The city welcomed him in ways the palace never could.

Calicut was a living mosaic. Its streets sang with colour: the vermilion of dried chillies spread like fire across mats; the indigo of dyers who laughed and scrubbed their arms blue to the elbows; the golden sheen of turmeric-stained hands, lifted in prayer or trade.

The air buzzed with strange, beautiful syllables, the scents of cumin and jackfruit, jasmine and smoke. There were temples that sounded like music, mosques that smelled like ink and rain, shrines shaded by mango trees where women left small garlands and whispered to stone.

Tomas wandered with the easy grace of one who had forgotten his homeland, if only for an hour. He was near the docks again when he first saw the boy.

He couldn't have been more than eleven or twelve, barefoot, lean as a reed, sun-polished and grinning. He was perched on the prow of a moored fishing boat, tying knots with the precision of a man twice his age.

"Strong rope," Tomas said casually, in Portuguese. The boy looked up, puzzled.

Tomas tried again, miming the twist of the rope and offering a half-smile. "Good knot."

The boy squinted. "*Nalla...* good. Very strong." He thumped the rope. "Wind like lion, no break." Tomas crouched beside the boat, intrigued. "You speak Portuguese?"

The boy tapped his temple. "Little. Ship men say. I listen." "What's your name?"

He hesitated. "Paru. But call me Kannan." Tomas nodded. "Kannan."

The boy looked pleased. "You? Name?"

"Tomas."

"Kannan and Tomaas," he said, mangling the syllables but grinning as if it was a song.

There was an awkward silence. Two boys of different worlds, linked by a handful of words and a shared nearness to the sea.

Then, without warning, Kannan stood and gestured wildly toward the boat's mast. "Laskar!" he declared, puffing out his chest. "One day. Like you."

Tomas laughed. "You want to be a laskar?"

Kannan nodded so fiercely his curls bounced. "Go big ship. Big wind. Far land. Far stars."

Tomas studied the boy. He was all bones and brightness, wrapped in a torn tunic, and yet something about him rang true. A hunger not for food, but for movement. For the edge of the map.

"You've never been outside Calicut?"

Kannan shook his head. "But I see stars. Same stars you see." Tomas smiled, humbled by the poetry.

They sat on the dock together as the sun slid low. Tomas carved a small boat from driftwood with his belt knife. Kannan watched every motion, eyes wide. When

Tomas handed it to him, the boy didn't speak. He just held it like a talisman, then tucked it into his tunic and pressed his palms together in thanks.

Later that night, Tomas returned to the ship and found Diogo spinning tales to a circle of sailors.

"They say the palace walls are hollow," Diogo was saying, "and if you speak too loud, the Zamorin hears you in his bath."

The men laughed, but Tomas barely heard. His mind was still at the docks. With the boy, and the dream he carried.

In the captain's quarters, Da Gama sat writing letters for the return fleet. There was tension around his mouth, a tautness in his spine.

"They delayed the meeting again," Da Gama said without looking up.

He sat at his writing desk, surrounded by scrolls and half-finished letters, but his eyes had long drifted from ink to uncertainty. He was not writing now. He was listening.

"Because they're still watching us," Tomas replied, leaning lightly against the frame of the captain's quarters. "Still deciding if we're visitors or invaders."

Da Gama met his gaze.

He was quiet for a moment longer than he needed to be. Then he said, "And what do you think?"

Tomas shrugged, but there was a solemnity behind it. "I think we're something stranger. We're questions. Ghosts from stories they haven't written yet."

The words struck Da Gama not for their cleverness, but for their stillness. In the candlelight, Tomas looked less like a sailor and more like a mirror. Reflecting the land back at him, letting it shape the contours of his thought.

Da Gama felt something tighten in his chest. A realisation he hadn't wanted to name.

He'd begun to trust this young man. This stowaway, with salt in his heart and poetry in his silences. Not because Tomas obeyed. But because he observed. He wandered where Da Gama could not, spoke less but listened more. And unlike the others, he did not seem driven by conquest or coin.

He remembered the first weeks aboard. The younger man always scribbling into his water-stained notebook, charting not just stars but birds, sounds, expressions on native faces. While others drank or spat or scowled at unknown customs, Tomas watched with the reverence of someone seeking to understand, not just survive.

There was danger in that softness. But also, perhaps, its own kind of strength.

"You've seen more of the city than I have," Da Gama said finally, his voice quieter now, less command than confession.

Tomas nodded.

"Then tell me. What do they say of us?"

"That we came too far," Tomas said. "That we brought steel and stories. And that some of us, might be listening."

The next morning, Tomas returned to the dock.

Kannan was waiting, barefoot as always, with two ripe mangoes and a grin that stretched across the sea.

They traded words now, piecing sentences together like shards of broken pottery. *Fish, wind, west, elephant, star.* They repeated each other's words with laughter and exaggerated gestures until meaning bloomed between them like a monsoon flower. The city was their classroom. Their teacher: patience.

Kannan showed Tomas how to crack a coconut with three sharp knocks against a stone, the trick being to find the lines hidden in the shell. Tomas, in turn, taught Kannan to whistle with two fingers. A long, sharp call that startled birds from rooftops and made the vendors turn.

They played games with stones and shells, drawing circles in the dust and inventing rules neither fully understood. They sketched maps in the sand with driftwood: imagined lands, secret harbours, treasure trails. One day, Kannan drew a shape and said, "My village." Tomas drew a star next to it. "I'll go there," he said. Kannan beamed.

They shared sweet rice wrapped in banana leaves, licking jaggery from their fingers, laughing as a monkey tried to steal a mango from Kannan's satchel. One afternoon, Kannan took Tomas through a spice lane so narrow even the sunlight folded its arms. The air shimmered with cardamom, pepper, turmeric, and something smoky that Tomas couldn't name. "This," Kannan said proudly, "is smell of Calicut."

Tomas gave him a stub of charcoal from the ship's stores. Kannan used it to draw a sailboat on a whitewashed wall. A small boy with curly hair stood on the deck, pointing toward a distant shore. Below it, he scrawled a word in Malayalam.

"What does it say?" Tomas asked. Kannan grinned. "Dream."

Sometimes, they didn't speak at all. They just sat at the edge of the quay, watching dhows come and go, the sea a shimmering mirror of the sky above. Kannan would chew tamarind pods and hum songs Tomas didn't know. Tomas would watch the boy's face and think of his tannery mates left behind in Portugal, of stories never told.

It was enough.

But Calicut was not just spices and serenity. The same afternoon, as the sun began to tilt westward and the scent of frying jackfruit fritters mingled with burning camphor, Tomas wandered into a busier quarter of the market. He had just bartered for a string of glass beads when he felt the weight of a gaze.

A man stood half in shadow beneath a crimson awning, his posture too still for a shopper. He wore a silk turban the colour of indigo twilight, and around his wrist was tied a thin red thread, the kind Tomas had seen on the priests in the temple courtyards. He stepped forward, moving without hurry, his sandals silent on the packed earth. His eyes were ink-black, unreadable.

"You walk like a man who wants no trouble," the stranger said smoothly, in Portuguese that was almost too perfect, too deliberate.

Tomas's heart skipped once, but he kept his voice even. "And if I do?"

The man tilted his head, the corners of his mouth curling. Neither a smile nor a threat, but something that echoed of both.

"Then you should stop speaking to children who know things they shouldn't."

The words struck like a cold wind through cloth. Tomas felt his spine straighten, his mind already tracing back every step, every whispered word, every smile shared with Kannan.

"Kannan?" he asked quietly, almost without breath.

The man stepped closer, until Tomas could smell the faintest hint of cloves and jasmine oil. "The boy sees too much," he said, almost lazily. "The city watches through many eyes, *Senhor*. Not all of them are kind."

His tone was not overtly threatening. It was worse. It was bored. As if he had delivered a message, and its implications were already out of his hands. He turned before Tomas could respond, slipping sideways into a clot of saffron-robed pilgrims. A moment later, he was gone. Vanished into the human tide of the market, as if the air itself had swallowed him.

Tomas stood frozen for a beat longer, the weight of the encounter settling on his shoulders like humid air before a storm. The market moved around him in rhythm: bells rang, coins clinked, someone called out prices for turmeric and tamarind, but the world felt suddenly off-key.

He glanced back the way he had come. In the distance, the minarets shimmered in the afternoon light, and a single crow flew across the sky, its cry slicing through the din. Somewhere near the dock, a boy might still be waiting with a grin and two more mangoes.

But Tomas was no longer sure who was watching whom.

That evening, Tomas didn't go to the docks. Instead, he sat alone beneath the shadow of a temple tree, tracing constellations on his palm.

Da Gama found him there.

"You've gone quiet," the captain said.

"I'm starting to hear things," Tomas replied. "Real things."

They sat in silence, the way only those who've crossed oceans can. No words, only the wind.

After a while, Tomas said, "There's a boy who wants to be a sailor. And a man who wants him to disappear."

Da Gama looked at him carefully. "What will you do?"

"Teach him what I can. Protect him, if I must."

Da Gama nodded. "Then we are both playing dangerous games."

"I know."

Above them, fireflies blinked like stars that had dropped to earth. Somewhere nearby, a conch blew. Distant thunder rolled.

And the city held its breath.

CHAPTER ELEVEN

The Fire Between

At dawn, the sky over Calicut bruised purple. Smoke rose somewhere in the west of the city. Low, smudged, not yet urgent. From the deck of the *Sao Gabriel*, Da Gama watched it curl like a warning, his face unreadable.

Tomas had been ashore again. Kannan had taken him inland this time, beyond the scent of spice markets and the gleam of temples, to places the map didn't name. They slipped through alleys where the walls wept with moss and the air smelled of damp stone, tamarind, and old smoke.

A quarter where smiths hammered iron into song. Each clang a bell that echoed against tiled roofs and stirred pigeons from the eaves. The heat shimmered off their forges, and the sharp tang of molten metal stung Tomas's throat.

Nearby, potters worked at spinning wheels under awnings of stitched palm leaves, their fingers dancing through clay, wrists flecked in ochre and red dust, murmuring lullabies to their creations. The earth smelled alive here. Sunbaked and wet all at once.

They passed a narrow courtyard where a shrine stood beneath a gnarled neem tree, its bark wrapped in red threads and copper coins pressed into its trunk. A diya flickered in a clay niche, its flame wavering in the breeze like it, too, was listening. Incense curled upward in thin spirals, and the air buzzed. Not just with flies or heat, but with something older, watching.

"You said this part wasn't safe," Tomas murmured.

Kannan shrugged. "Safe is what you call a place after you leave it."

They ducked beneath a row of hanging fabrics and into the narrow courtyard of a weaver's house. The walls were close, sun-dappled. From within came the click and clatter of looms. Kannan motioned him to wait. He vanished through a door and returned moments later with a bundle wrapped in linen.

"For your captain," he said. "They say kings wear gold. But Calicut wraps its kings in thread."

Inside the bundle was a length of brocade. Not ostentatious. Beautiful. Meticulous. Stories told in silk.

Tomas swallowed. "Thank you."

Kannan grinned, and then, uncharacteristically, grew quiet. "You should not come back tomorrow."

"Why?"

The boy hesitated. "They say... the temple astrologers have seen a sword in the sky." Tomas tilted his head.

"What does that mean?"

"Trouble." Kannan's voice was low. "And people looking for someone to blame."

By noon, trouble had a face. It came not with shouting, but with silk and sandals. In the shaded peristyle of the palace gardens, where Da Gama had been invited to wait under a canopy of flowering flame trees, a courtier approached. Neither hurried nor idle, bearing the weight of discretion.

The man was a Brahmin scholar, his forehead marked with ash, his eyes shadowed by sleeplessness and the burden of news. He bowed with measured grace.

"Admiral," he said in careful Portuguese, "your presence honours us."

Da Gama inclined his head, patient but unyielding. "You come with words." "There has been... a complication."

"What kind?"

"Two merchants in the northern quarter claimed injury. They say it was your men."

"And were they?"

The Brahmin hesitated. "They are not to be found. But the tale spreads quickly. And the shape of a tale, as you know, matters more than its spine."

"Witnesses?"

"Many. However, their truths do not align." "And the Zamorin?" Da Gama asked.

The scholar looked away, toward the marbled colonnades and the slow rustle of garden wind chimes. "He listens. To the markets, the astrologers, the drums in the temple. But listening is not the same as believing."

Da Gama's expression did not change, but the wind shifted in his chest. "And you?"

The Brahmin met his eyes. "I believe a spark may be no one's fault. But the fire? That belongs to all who watched it light."

Meanwhile, Tomas found himself watched.

Not by palace guards or hawk-eyed merchants. Not even the market spies who loitered beneath banyan trees, whispering into lime-stained palms. No. This shadow had a name he did not know and a scent he could not forget. The man with the clove-scented turban and red thread around his wrist appeared again, as if conjured by heat and questions.

This time, he found Tomas alone beneath the heavy boughs of a fig tree, where Kannan had gone off chasing a street procession with painted bulls and flute music. The man sat beside him without a word, as though they'd planned it. As though he belonged.

Tomas tensed. "You again."

"I never left," the man said calmly. "Only waitcd for the right silence." Tomas studied him. "What do you want?"

"To finish what I began. And to tell you the part I didn't say."

Tomas's fingers brushed the pouch at his waist. Not in fear, but memory. "Go on."

The man tilted his head. "The boy, Kannan, he is not merely curious. He is being watched. Not just by me. Not just by the court. There are those in the city who trade in futures. In information. And he, poor soul, sees too much and speaks too freely."

Tomas's face darkened. "Is that a threat?"

"It's a warning," the man said. "There's a difference. One bleeds quicker."

He reached into his robe and took out a small figurine. An elephant carved from black stone, its eyes inlaid with ruby dust. "This was found in the quarters of a merchant who went missing last week. He dealt in more than spices. The kind of knowledge Kannan gathers by accident." Tomas hesitated. "You think he's next?"

"I think," the man said, "that those who wield power in this city; traders, priests, sailors, princes, do not like children who walk between worlds."

Tomas studied the figurine. "And me?"

"You're a ghost in their stories. They haven't decided if you're an omen or a mistake." The man stood, dusting his robes. "You care about the boy. So do I. But we play different games."

He stepped back into the street, the sun flaring off his turban like firelight. Then he paused and turned.

"When the drums beat tonight in the northern quarter," he said softly, "stay close to the ones who still listen. And ask your captain again, why Calicut?"

And just like that, he disappeared into the crowd. Into the scent of saffron smoke, into the unanswered questions the city had begun to whisper louder than ever before.

The council that evening on the *Sao Gabriel* was tense.

Vitor, the first mate, slammed his cup down. "Three days of delays, and now this accusation? They want to bleed us dry of gifts and goad us into mistake."

"They want us to choose," Da Gama said, voice even. "To be traders. Or invaders." "And what are we?"

Tomas was in the corner, listening. When the silence stretched, he spoke. "I met someone. Said we were neither."

They turned to him. Da Gama didn't interrupt.

"He said we were... shadows from stories they haven't written yet." Vitor scoffed. "Poetry won't get us pepper."

"No," Tomas said. "But maybe it'll keep us from being the fire that burns the tale before it's told."

Da Gama's eyes stayed on Tomas. Then, slowly, he nodded. "We'll send a gift to the palace tomorrow. Not gold. Not guns. Something else."

"What?" asked one of the lieutenants. "Stories," Da Gama said. "In the form of silk."

The next day, Kannan didn't meet Tomas at the docks. Instead, a garland of marigolds hung from the post where they usually met. Tomas didn't know what it meant. A sign of friendship? Or warning?

He walked alone.

The city felt different. Louder in some places, quieter in others. Like a breath held. In the spice district, a man bumped into him too hard. Not an accident. In the alleyway past the temple, two boys stopped talking when he passed. He didn't go far. He didn't need to. The city was speaking. Just not in words he knew.

Back aboard the ship, Da Gama stood by the rail with his arms folded. "They postponed the audience again," he said.

Tomas said nothing. "Why?" Da Gama asked.

Tomas looked toward the city. "Because they're waiting to see what kind of storm we are." "And what kind are we?"

"Not the kind that brings rain," Tomas replied. "Not yet."

That evening, a letter arrived.

No seal. No sender. Just a folded square of palm-leaf parchment, tied with a red thread. It was addressed to no one in particular, but Da Gama opened it.

Inside was a short message, written in firm, slanted Portuguese:

The boy is in danger. Not from us. From those who would use his voice to silence yours.

Da Gama read it three times before handing it to Tomas. "He's more than just a boy," he said quietly. "Isn't he?" Tomas didn't answer. He didn't need to.

The captain turned back to his maps.

"Tell him to be careful," he said. "Tell him... we'll find a way."

In the courtyard of the old weaver's house, the loom was still. The colours had been taken down. The shadows were long.

Kannan sat cross-legged, drawing shapes in the dust with a twig. When he saw Tomas, his eyes lit up; but only for a moment.

"Someone came," the boy said. "Asking questions." Tomas crouched beside him. "About what?" "About you. About the ship. About... what I see."

Tomas took a deep breath. "You don't have to speak to them." "I didn't."

"Good."

"But they'll come back."

"I know."

They sat in silence. Then Tomas reached into his satchel and pulled out a folded piece of parchment. It was a map. Crude. Unfinished. Lines drawn by memory, not compass. Kannan looked at it, puzzled.

"It's the way from your house to the shore," Tomas said. "And from there to our ship. If you need to find us. Fast."

Kannan touched the lines like they were threads. "And if they catch me before?"

Tomas hesitated. "Then they'll find someone who won't break. Because you're stronger than they think."

Kannan looked up. "You sound like you believe it."

"I do."

And this time, it wasn't a strategy. It was truth.

CHAPTER TWELVE

The Needle and the Flame

The rains had come again in the night. Not the heavy kind that lashed against sails and soured temperaments, but the softer drizzle that beaded on leaves and turned the red earth fragrant. Tomas woke to that scent, the musky breath of a land steeped in secrets and soaked in spice. The harbour was a grey smear, the ships at anchor gently creaking like beasts at rest.

But the city was already awake.

From the upper decks of the *Sao Gabriel*, Tomas watched the shoreline flicker into life. Fishwives in bright cottons hawked at the edge of the wharf, their bangles catching the light. A line of bullocks moved with a stubborn rhythm, dragging carts laden with *areca* nuts and tamarind barrels. He saw a washerman slap linen against the stones near the canal's mouth. It made a rhythmic sound, like a drummer greeting the day. A gull cawed. Somewhere inland, a temple bell sang.

By the time Tomas reached the city, the clouds had lifted just enough to bathe Calicut in a muted gold. The streets shimmered from the night's rain, puddles holding distorted reflections of minarets, tiled domes, and the swollen green of the jackfruit trees.

Kannan was waiting.

He had a slingshot tucked in his waistband and a mischievous glint that never quite left his eyes. Today he wore a shirt two sizes too large and no shoes. In one hand, he carried a folded fan made of palm leaves; in the other, a warm bundle of breakfast. *Puttu*, wrapped in banana leaf and still steaming.

They shared it sitting under the shade of a copper-podded tree, the city yawning around them. "Eat, firangi," Kannan said with mock seriousness. "No trade without food."

Tomas smiled. Their words were still a jagged bridge. Broken, pieced together with signs and repetition. But by now it felt like a language of its own.

Kannan took him inland again, deeper than before. Past the markets painted in turmeric and sunlight, past the courtyards where parrots shrieked from hanging cages. Past the last of the spice stalls and the sea's salted breath. They entered a neighbourhood of narrow lanes where craftsmen ruled.

Here, smiths hunched over anvils, bare-chested and glistening, coaxing blade and buckle from fire. Sparks flew like fireflies in daylight. Hammers rose and fell in perfect synchrony, like a forge-led orchestra. Next door, a potter's wheel spun steadily, clay blossoming beneath the potter's hands like a coiled lotus. His arms were streaked in ochre, his forehead marked in ash.

Kannan motioned for silence and led Tomas around the back of a building where a neem tree stood. It was crooked, gnarled and old, its bark festooned with red threads tied by countless hands.

Beneath it sat a tiny shrine. No taller than a child. Painted white and garlanded with wilted jasmine. The stone deity inside was faceless, only a smooth oval of black rock. But someone had lit a wick before it, and the flame danced in the breeze.

"This god?" Tomas asked softly. Kannan shrugged. "All gods. Or none."

They stood in silence, the hum of a nearby loom folding into the quiet like a hidden breath.

A woman passed with a basket of marigolds on her head. A boy dragged a goat on a frayed rope. A vendor shouted about sesame oil. The air smelled of wet clay, roasted gram, incense, and something burning sweet. Maybe sugarcane stalks in an open fire.

"Why show me this?" Tomas asked, finally.

Kannan drew a rough shape in the dust, a circle, with a line running through it. Then he tapped Tomas's chest and repeated the gesture.

"Inside," he said.

Tomas didn't answer. He only nodded. It was enough. That afternoon, the mood shifted.

There was talk near the temple square. Da Gama had been summoned again, not to the palace, but to the garden court. An indirect snub in courtly language. Rumours crackled like dry leaves. Some said Portuguese sailors had been found bartering illegally for gold. Others whispered of a stolen idol, though none could say which temple or whose God.

At the ship, Da Gama paced the deck, flanked by the ship's officers and a scribe who could barely keep up with his dictations. He looked older, suddenly. Wearier.

When Tomas returned with mud still clinging to his boots, Da Gama turned sharply. "Where have you been?"

"Walking. Learning."

"We may not have that luxury much longer." Tomas stepped closer. "What happened?"

"The market incident was only the start. Someone is stoking fear. Someone with influence."

Tomas hesitated, then said, "I spoke again with the man in the turban. He wasn't warning me anymore. He was choosing sides."

Da Gama stared. "And what side is that?"

"One that believes the boy is more than just a boy."

Da Gama's lips tightened. "The city is a chessboard. And it plays with live pieces." "You think the boy is in danger?"

"I think we all are. But him most of all."

At that moment, a runner arrived. A message, hastily scrawled in a local script and sealed with indigo dye. Tomas caught the first two words: *Temple fire.*

He looked up. "Where?"

"Near the neem shrine," Da Gama said, reading the translation.

Tomas didn't wait. He was already moving.

He ran past the vendors, past the tailors' row and the spice presses, past the coconut-sellers and lantern-men. The air felt tight. Crowds thinned where the smoke began. Near the neem tree, chaos bloomed.

The shrine still stood. Barely. But the neem tree above it had been scorched, its ancient bark charred in streaks, as if a cruel hand had painted it with fire. Someone had tried to burn it down. The smoke still hung low in the air, clinging to the under leaves like mourning shrouds. Soot crawled up the trunk like creeping ivy, blackening the red threads tied there by generations of silent prayers. Many had burned through, curling into brittle ash that floated down like dying feathers.

The smell was thick and bitter. The acrid sting of smouldered oil and sacred cloth, cut with the faint, unmistakable tang of cow dung fire. Tomas coughed, eyes watering. The sanctity of the place had been violated. Not just a tree or a shrine, but something older, something ancestral. It felt like walking into a temple desecrated mid-offering.

Kannan was there, standing just beyond the scorched roots. His face was pale beneath the layer of dust. His eyes were wide. Not just with fear, but with disbelief. As if a truth he'd trusted had just been shattered. He held a small clay vessel in both hands, cradling it like a wounded bird. The wick inside it still burned, a thin, flickering flame defying the ruin around it. Smoke spiralled from it, curling like a ghost toward the ruined threads above.

He didn't speak. He didn't need to.

Tomas immediately understood. This was no random act. It was a message. A threat cloaked in fire and silence.

"What happened?" Tomas asked, breathless.

Kannan didn't answer. Just pointed to a figure running away. A youth in fine robes, face wrapped, carrying something hidden beneath his shawl.

Not a thief. A message. Not an accident. A spark.

The crowd was growing now. Voices rose. Someone shouted about curses. Another spat in the dirt. Tomas reached out and gently placed a hand on Kannan's shoulder. "Come. We should go."

The boy looked at the scorched offerings, then back at the foreigner who, somehow, understood. They turned together and slipped into the smoke.

Far above, in the garden courts of the palace, a plan was taking root. Not merely of trade, but of dominion. The kind of quiet, deliberate design that grows beneath silk words and golden gestures. A plot drawn not just on maps but in margins. In glances. In whispers traded between courtiers and commanders.

And far below, in the labyrinthine belly of the city, a story was catching fire. Not the kind scribed on palm leaves or sung in courts, but a living, breathing tale that slipped through cracks and settled in the lungs of common folk.

It spread with the hush of suspicion and the roar of anger. It moved faster than the spice carts, and slower than truth. And it would not be doused easily.

Not with water. Not with silence.

Not even with blood.

Embers Beneath the Ash

The sun had barely crested the horizon, casting a golden hue over Calicut, when the city stirred with a restless energy. The scent of spices and clove mingled with the briny tang of the sea, wafting through the narrow alleys and bustling bazaars. Fishermen hauled in their morning catch, their nets glistening with silver scales, while merchants unfurled vibrant textiles, their colours rivalling the dawn sky.

In the heart of this awakening city, Tomas stood beside Kannan, both gazing at the charred remains of the neem tree shrine. The once-sacred threads, now reduced to ashes, whispered tales of desecration and warning. Kannan's grip on the clay vessel tightened, its flickering flame a fragile beacon amidst the ruin.

"Who would do this?" Tomas murmured, his voice tinged with disbelief.

Kannan's eyes, usually filled with mischief, were now shadowed with fear. "Not who," he replied softly, "but why."

The city's undercurrents had shifted. What once flowed with the quiet rhythm of trade and ritual now pulsed with something sharper, more volatile. Whispers of unrest threaded through the alleys like smoke, curling beneath shutters, brushing past the ears of hawkers and priests alike. They were carried on the wind like the distant echo of war drums. Low, steady, and ominous.

In tea stalls and under banyan trees, words were spoken in hushed tones. Eyes darted. Hands trembled slightly as they exchanged coins. The incident at the shrine was not seen as random or petty. It was too precise, too symbolic. A sacred tree blackened by flame. Threads of prayer scorched and dangling like torn skin. In this act, the city read more than desecration. It read defiance. A warning. A wound.

It was not just smoke that rose from the base of the neem tree. It was history, myth, belonging. And now, suspicion clung to every corner like damp. People looked over their shoulders, not knowing if they should fear the foreigner or their own neighbour. Simmering grievances, bruised pride, and the weight of unseen power, had now begun to boil.

This was no longer just a city of spices and song. Something darker had begun to rise from its belly. And it would not be stilled with silence.

Back aboard the Sao Gabriel, Vasco da Gama paced the deck, his brow furrowed in contemplation. The news of the shrine's desecration had reached him swiftly, and he sensed the delicate balance of power teetering. The Zamorin's court, once a place of cautious diplomacy, now bristled with suspicion and veiled threats.

"We must tread carefully," da Gama advised his officers. "Our presence here is both opportunity and provocation."

Tomas, upon returning to the ship, relayed his encounter at the shrine. Da Gama listened intently, his gaze fixed on the horizon.

"This city is a tapestry," Tomas concluded, "each thread connected. Pull one, and the whole unravels."

Da Gama nodded. "Then we must ensure our threads are woven with care."

As days passed, the atmosphere in Calicut grew increasingly charged. Markets buzzed with rumours, and the once-welcoming faces of locals now bore expressions of caution. The Portuguese presence, initially a novelty, had become a focal point of contention.

One evening, Kannan led Tomas through a labyrinth of alleyways to a secluded courtyard. There, an elderly man awaited them, his eyes sharp despite his age. He introduced himself as Ravi, a scholar and keeper of local lore.

"The shrine's desecration," Ravi began without preamble, "is a symbol. It signifies a breach, not just of sanctity, but of trust."

Tomas leaned forward. "Trust between whom? Us and them?"

"Between the old ways and the new," Ravi explained. "The arrival of foreign powers disrupts the equilibrium.

Some see it as progress; others, as a threat."

Ravi's words resonated with Tomas. He realised that their mission was not merely about trade or exploration, but about navigating the intricate web of cultural and political dynamics.

The Zamorin had not yet spoken.

In the shaded chamber that opened to the palace gardens, the court had gathered in uneasy silence. Incense burned in thin, crooked trails that twisted toward the open sky. But even its fragrance could not mask the tension that coiled in the air. Outside, the cries of mynas and the rustle of palm leaves sounded distant. Almost irrelevant. Inside, the murmur of silk against stone, of breath held too long, filled the space.

This was no formal durbar. There were no garlands, no drums. Only senior advisors and ministers, some summoned in haste, others having arrived long before sunrise, sensing the storm to come. At the centre, the Zamorin sat cross-legged, his expression carved from calm. But his stillness was not serenity. It was watchfulness. He listened, eyes fixed on the floor, as his court debated the future of his kingdom.

"The shrine was no accident," said Keshavan Namboodiri, his voice tight. He was a temple trustee, respected and feared, his white beard yellowed with turmeric. "It was a message. An insult wrapped in fire. And still, we let them walk our streets?"

Ravi Valiya Kurup, the chief of the harbour guilds, scoffed. "And if we throw them out? Then what? The Venetians will laugh behind their masks. The Ottomans will tighten their grip on the Red Sea routes. Do we crawl back to them for every grain of pepper?"

"Trade is not slavery," said a younger courtier, his voice rising above his station. "And profit is not peace. These men, these... strangers, they speak with silver, but walk with steel. Even now, they pry into our customs, our people. A boy was seen speaking with them. A mere child!"

Others murmured in agreement. Some, in dissent.

"Are we to fear every foreigner who enters our markets?" asked Balan Menon, the elder naval commander, weather-burned and straight-backed despite the heat. "The city has always been a meeting place of winds. Of strangers. That is our strength."

"But these winds reek of smoke," muttered the commander of the palace guards, his hand resting on the pommel of his dagger. "I say we watch them more closely. Assign shadows to their shadows. No move without our knowing."

A silence followed that suggestion. The kind that slips in when a room edges toward danger.

From the shadows near the carved pillars, a soft voice broke through. "Their ships are too large to be just merchant vessels," said the eunuch court advisor. He was known for seeing what others did not. "And their eyes carry the weight of maps. Not of wonder, but of conquest."

There it was. The word no one had yet spoken aloud. The Zamorin lifted his gaze, finally.

Not to speak. Not yet. But to look. Slowly, deliberately. At each voice that had spoken. Measuring not just their words, but what those words carried: fear, ambition, loyalty, uncertainty.

A flicker of motion from his left. The royal astrologer had stepped forward, not to speak, but to place a small copper dish at the foot of the dais. Inside it: a palm leaf scroll, tied with indigo thread. An omen reading, drawn from the stars the night the shrine burned.

The Zamorin did not touch it. Instead, he turned to his inner circle, his voice low, but unwavering. "We have hosted travellers for centuries. Some stayed. Some fled. Some tried to rule."

He paused. The jasmine above him stirred in a breathless gust. "But never before has my city felt watched from within." More silence. Even the birds outside had quieted.

"My decision must be precise," he said. "And final. To banish them is to close a door the world will not let us reopen. To accept them blindly is to offer our throat to a smiling knife."

He leaned back, hands resting lightly on his knees.

"So tell me again, each of you. What do we do? Not with our anger, but with our future?"

And thus, the council resumed. This time, slower, deeper. The words were heavier now, shaped not by impulse, but by consequence. And in every corner of the court, from those craving profit to those sensing betrayal, the truth grew clear:

The days of hospitality were ending. The days of decision had begun.

As tensions escalated, a clandestine meeting took place between da Gama and a representative of the Zamorin. The room was small and windowless. Lined with sandalwood shelves heavy with scrolls. Hidden away from the grandeur of court and the clamour of the harbour. Only a single oil lamp lit the chamber, its flame flickering against walls that had heard centuries of secrets.

The envoy, a Brahmin scholar robed in plain cotton and marked with sacred ash, entered with quiet authority. He did not sit until invited, nor did he waste time with pleasantries. His voice was calm, but each word carried the weight of deliberation.

"The Zamorin seeks assurance," the scholar stated. "That your intentions are honourable and that your presence will not disrupt the harmony of our land."

There was no threat in his tone. Yet no doubt that the consequences of dishonesty would be severe.

Da Gama responded with measured words, each syllable chosen with care, polished by diplomacy. He spoke of shared prosperity, of mutual respect, of the spice roads that could bind two oceans rather than split them. He nodded to the wisdom of the Zamorin, praised the civility of the people, and offered gestures of goodwill.

But beneath the surface, both men understood the fragility of the moment. It was not simply trade that hung in balance. But the future of two worlds brushing against one another, wary of the heat between them. A single misstep, a misread gesture, could fracture more than alliances. It could spill blood.

The silence that followed was not empty. It brimmed with the knowledge that the next few days would determine whether this meeting had built a bridge. Or lit a fuse.

In the days that followed, a series of incidents further strained relations. A Portuguese sailor was accused of theft; a local merchant's warehouse mysteriously caught fire. Each event added fuel to the growing fire of mistrust.

Tomas, caught between two worlds, sought solace in his friendship with Kannan. Together, they navigated the complexities of their respective cultures, finding common ground in shared experiences and mutual respect.

One evening, as they sat beneath a starlit sky, Kannan turned to Tomas. "Change is coming," he said. "We must decide whether to resist it or shape it."

Tomas nodded, understanding the weight of his friend's words. The path ahead was uncertain, but he was determined to walk it with integrity and purpose.

Calicut held its breath. Not as a city conquered, but as a city watching, weighing, and waiting to choose what kind of future it would allow through its gates.

CHAPTER FOURTEEN

A Spark in the Courtyard

The morning after the meeting with the envoy, a silence lay heavy over Calicut. Not the calm of peace, but the breath held before a storm.

Da Gama stood at the edge of the deck, his knuckles white against the railing. From the water, the city looked golden and still. But he could feel the temperature shifting. Not in the air, but in the glances of the guards. The tone of the translators. The days had grown tighter. The rituals, more formal. He was no longer an honoured guest. He was an equation to be solved, or a problem to be removed.

Below, in the maze of narrow lanes, another current pulsed. Tomas walked through the city with his shoulders tighter than usual, Kannan beside him with less of a bounce in his step. The incident at the shrine had left a bruise. People still visited the neem tree, still lit small oil lamps and tied fresh threads, but their faces bore wariness instead of reverence. The scorched bark was now half-covered in white paste, as if to erase the memory. But it lingered.

Whispers clung to Tomas wherever he went now. Half-words in Malayalam that paused when he passed. He didn't always need Kannan to translate. Suspicion had its own language.

In the palace, the tension had spilled past veils and walls.

The queen mother had summoned her astrologer twice in one day. Courtiers passed one another in corridors like birds wary of storm clouds. Every discussion was measured. And watched.

A younger prince, Bhaskaran Thampuran, had begun gathering supporters among the merchant guilds. "Trade with the far lands brings power," he had said, loud enough to be overheard. "Power must not be feared. It must be mastered."

But older voices resisted. "Foreigners are waves. They come with promise and leave with silt," said a grey-bearded Namboothiri. "This land is old. Older than the names of these sea-people."

There were murmurs of Portuguese ships sighted farther south. Of local rulers in Cochin and Cannanore watching carefully, weighing loyalties. The spice routes trembled under invisible strain.

That evening, as the last sun glazed the palace tiles in amber, a sharp cry rose from the outer courtyards.

It was followed by a commotion. Shouts, the clash of spears against marble. Tomas, who had been walking back from the stables, turned on instinct and ran toward the sound, Kannan at his heels.

A group of men had forced their way through one of the smaller gates. No weapons were drawn, but their presence was challenge enough. Traders, by the look of them. *Mappilas*, their cotton robes marked by salt and sea. One held up a scroll. Another shouted in Arabic-accented Malayalam.

"They say one of their people was attacked," a guard explained to a senior palace official, who had rushed to intercept.

"In the spice quarter. They claim a foreign sailor took what was not his."

Kannan tugged Tomas's sleeve. "They think it was one of your men," he whispered. "Maybe it wasn't. Or maybe it was."

Tomas's throat felt dry. "What will they do?"

Kannan's answer was too quiet to hear over the raised voices, but the look in his eyes was loud enough.

That night, Da Gama summoned Tomas.

"You've been among them," he said, voice clipped, face lit only by a swaying lantern. "What are they saying?"

Tomas hesitated. "That the city is listening now. That something's shifting." Da Gama frowned. "Do they think we'll leave?"

"Some hope. Some fear. Most don't know."

The captain was silent for a long time. Then he leaned forward, his expression unreadable. "We may not be given a choice. If things break, I'll need eyes where I can't be. You've earned the boy's trust. Use it."

Tomas stiffened. "Kannan's not a tool."

Da Gama's gaze sharpened. "He's a thread into this place. He hears what others don't, walks where we can't follow, speaks the language of back doors and whispered names. I need that thread."

"To do what?"

"To find out who's stoking this fire. Who's trying to turn the city against us. I want names. Streets. Patterns. Not just sentiment."

Tomas looked down, jaw tight. "He's just a boy."

"And boys have changed the course of kingdoms," Da Gama replied. "He won't be harmed. But you'll guide him. You'll decide what you hear, and what you bring to me."

Tomas turned away. The lantern's flame flickered in his eyes, casting shifting shadows across his face.

"If I do this," he said slowly, "there's no turning back." Da Gama didn't answer. He didn't need to.

The silence between them was not emptiness. It was the edge of a blade.

Two days later, the spice quarter exploded.

Not with fire or blood, but voices. A trader was dragged from his stall, accused of overcharging a Portuguese sailor. He claimed innocence. Bystanders claimed provocation. The guards hesitated. A sandal hit someone's back. Someone pushed back. Then it turned.

No deaths. But bruises. Broken pottery. Spices spilled like blood.

By nightfall, the Zamorin's council was again in session. Not behind curtains, but in the open, for once. The public court.

Tomas and Kannan watched from a terrace alcove. The dais shimmered in lamplight, gold and sandalwood scent masking the sweat beneath silks.

Arguments rippled like heatwaves.

"This is no longer about trade," thundered one minister. "This is about the rhythm of our city. Its breath. You do not dance with someone who counts every step."

"We cannot pretend they will vanish," countered a courtier aligned with Bhaskaran Thampuran. "If we turn them away, they will return with teeth."

"They already have teeth," said a third, holding up a Portuguese blade confiscated days earlier. "And they sharpen them here."

The Zamorin listened, head bowed slightly. His fingers tapped slowly against the armrest of his carved ivory throne. He was not a young man. His eyes held the weight of decisions past and the ghost of futures not yet chosen.

He finally spoke.

"Calicut is a mirror. It shows what others bring to it. Gold, knowledge, worship, or war. The question before us is, what do they see in us? And what shall we become in their eyes?"

No one answered. Not right away.

That night, Tomas sat by the sea, where the ships rocked gently and the wind no longer sang. The hush of the water was deceptive. Like a breath held too long.

He had barely spoken since returning from the captain's quarters. The words Da Gama had spoken still clung to him, sharp-edged and unresolved. *Use the boy.* The phrase had echoed like an order and a betrayal all at once.

He remembered how the lantern had cast flickers across Da Gama's face. How the flame looked almost like it flinched when Tomas resisted.

Kannan sat beside him, legs drawn to his chest, arms looped around them. His face was drawn, older than it had looked just days ago. Ash still clung faintly to his nails from the shrine.

"You'll have to choose," the boy said suddenly, voice barely above the lap of the waves.

Tomas didn't look at him. His gaze was locked on the water, on the wavering lights of the city. "What do you mean?"

"Your captain. Or this place. You can't walk both roads when they split."

The words cut through the quiet. Tomas felt them settle into the hollow part of his chest. The part that had started to ache ever since they'd stepped ashore. He let out a breath, slow and uncertain.

"I didn't come here to spy," he said. "I came to learn. To witness. To witness new and adventurous places. Not to get caught up in intrigue and conspiracy."

Kannan tilted his head, watching him. "But now you have to choose."

Tomas nodded slowly. "Da Gama wants me to use you. To turn what you know into leverage. I told him no. But I don't think that matters anymore. The city is shifting, and he's pulling tight every thread he can reach."

Kannan looked away, out to sea.

"I used to lie on the roof and dream I was a Laskar," he said. "Not a prince. Not a hero. Just a sailor. Just enough coin to carry me to a coast I'd never seen. Salt in my hair and the sky my only ceiling."

He picked up a pebble and tossed it. It skipped once, then sank.

"But now? Everything's changing. Everyone's choosing sides. And dreams start to feel like lies someone else whispered to you when you were too young to know better."

Tomas turned to him, the heaviness pressing against his ribs. "If I could put you on a ship tonight and send you to that far coast, I would."

"But would you come with me?" Kannan asked quietly.

The question caught Tomas off guard. He hadn't considered it. Not really. He had thought of escape. But not with purpose. Not with company.

He looked at Kannan. The boy who had slipped through alleys and markets with the eyes of a hawk and the heart of a child trying to outrun a fire. His friend.

"I don't know," Tomas said honestly. "But I know I don't want to be the reason your dream dies." Kannan's lips curled, not quite into a smile. "Then don't."

A pause. Then Tomas said, "If it comes to it, if there's no choice left, we leave together. I'll get you on a boat. That's a promise."

Kannan nodded. "But not before we know what's coming."

And there it was. The shift. The unspoken agreement. They would stay. For now. To watch. To listen. To act, if they had to.

Somewhere inland, a drumbeat began. Not for dance. Not for festival. For warning. It was faint, but insistent. Like a pulse before a wound breaks open.

The stars watched silently as two silhouettes sat by the sea. Two souls balanced on the cusp of decision. And far behind them, the city breathed like something alive, waiting for morning to decide its shape.

Tomas closed his eyes.

Tomorrow would come. But tonight, they chose not to run.

CHAPTER FIFTEEN

The Match and the Sea

The air in Calicut had turned brittle.

By dawn, the harbour had changed. The Portuguese ships floated still, but not silent. Men moved in taut lines, tightening ropes, checking cannon placements, whispering orders with blades at their hips. No music rang from the decks. No laughter echoed over the water. Even the gulls seemed to caw more sharply, circling as though the sea itself had soured.

Inside the palace, the Zamorin's court gathered under a heavy hush. Silk rustled. Anklets chimed dully. The tiled floor, always cool, felt colder now beneath bare feet.

There was no ceremony to Da Gama's entrance. No trumpets. No gifts. He walked in with sand still on his boots and sea-wind still in his hair, trailed by two armed men who did not lower their gaze before the throne. The captain's jaw was set. He did not bow.

The Zamorin looked older that day. His face, always composed, bore lines more pronounced. Around him, his ministers sat in wary silence. Some drummed fingers on wooden armrests. Others clutched the hems of their robes.

"You requested this audience," the Zamorin said, voice even but tired. "Speak."

Da Gama didn't waste words. "Last night, two of our men were attacked while gathering provisions near the coast. One of them was knifed. We demand restitution."

Murmurs stirred among the courtiers. One minister, younger than the rest, leaned forward. "And what of the two Nairs taken from the spice quarter? Fishermen too?"

"They were detained for questioning," Da Gama said. "They interfered with our men. They're safe."

"No one interfered," another courtier snapped. "You seized them like cattle."

Da Gama's nostrils flared. "We have tolerated insult, slander, and spying. We came in peace. But we will not be threatened."

A sharp silence followed. The Zamorin said nothing. Only the flicker of a flame from a brass oil lamp moved between them, casting shadows like cracks across the wall.

Then the elder court scholar spoke, the same man who once warned of matches and fleets. "Peace," he said, slowly, "is not merely an absence of swords. It is the balance of breath. Yours has grown short."

Another voice cut in. "Trade must continue. These provocations... they benefit no one." "They benefit those who wish to rewrite rules," someone else murmured.

Da Gama took a breath. He turned to the Zamorin. "We leave at first tide. With or without your permission. And those we've detained, are leverage. Not prisoners. That will depend on your response."

He turned and walked out without waiting for reply. The doors did not creak shut. They slammed.

Word spread like fire in dry wind.

By midmorning, the streets were no longer murmuring. They roared. Tempers flared at market stalls. Fistfights broke out between strangers. Vendors packed up their wares in haste, shutters slammed shut, and temple drums beat not in rhythm, but in panic. The fishmongers no longer whispered. They shouted, eyes wide with fear. Children were yanked indoors by anxious mothers. The scent of incense mixed uneasily with the tang of smoke and sweat.

By midday, the harbour swelled with bodies. No longer curious, but furious. This was no simple gathering. It pulsed with something raw and dangerous. Men with painted foreheads carried sticks. Women stood with folded arms and clenched jaws. Even the elders, who usually calmed such storms, stood silent.

And all eyes were fixed on the ships. The Portuguese vessels bobbed in the bay like foreign beasts, too close, too armed. On their decks, movement had slowed. Muskets were checked. Eyes scanned the shore.

Below, onboard, the detained Nairs sat surrounded. Not by walls, but by unspoken threat. The fishermen, too, crouched like men waiting for lightning to strike. They spoke no Portuguese. The soldiers guarding them spoke no Malayalam. But silence is a language. And this one screamed.

Tomas stood at the edge of the captain's quarters, shoulders drawn tight, eyes flicking between the gathered officers and the charts spread across the table. The lanterns cast long shadows across Da Gama's face as he traced coastlines with an impatient finger.

"This city is growing bolder," one of the officers muttered. "The harbour swells with eyes. That crowd today... they weren't just watching."

"They were measuring us," said another, voice sharper. "Testing how far we'll bend." "We don't bend," Da Gama snapped. He didn't look up. "We break what must be broken."

Tomas shifted slightly, drawing breath, but said nothing. One of the lieutenants gestured toward the harbour map. "If this festers, we risk open confrontation. Our position is exposed. We hold hostages but no leverage."

Da Gama's jaw tightened. "We didn't start this. But we will finish it. Before the tide turns." "And if the city turns first?" someone asked.

The captain straightened, finally looking around. "Then we remind them who we are. And why we came."

In the corner, Tomas's fists curled at his sides. He felt the weight of the words like iron sinking in water. No one asked what happened to the city if that reminder came too late. And no one noticed when Tomas quietly stepped away.

Kannan found Tomas near the outer walls, where the breeze carried more than just salt. It carried the sharp, bitter tang of something lost. Smoke curled in slow ribbons from the quarter where the shrine had once stood. Ash danced in the wind like dying fireflies.

Tomas didn't hear him approach. He stood with his back to the city, staring at nothing, palms braced against the stone. The world behind his eyes was louder than the one in front.

"They've sealed parts of the city," Kannan said. His voice cracked with restraint. "Guards at every alley. The temple bells didn't ring this morning."

Tomas turned. Kannan's face was pale beneath the soot smudges. His lips were tight, but his eyes were boiling.

"I know," Tomas said, quietly.

"They're burning spices in the markets. Not yours, ours." Kannan's voice rose, trembled. "My mother stood there with a basket full of pepper and threw it into the flames. Because she said it's better than letting the sea-men profit from it. Do you understand what that means?"

Tomas opened his mouth but faltered. "I..."

"It means this isn't about trade anymore." Kannan took a step closer, his voice fierce. "It's about who we are.

What we'll give up just to not be ruled."

"I never came to rule anyone."

"No, but you came with those who did." Kannan's hands clenched at his sides. "And now look around you. There's a curfew in the fishermen's enclave. Women are praying with ashes on their foreheads. The city feels like it's holding its breath, and you..." he jabbed a finger at Tomas's chest "you still walk the in-between like it's safe ground. It's not."

Tomas flinched. "I didn't ask for this. I didn't plan any of this. I came here to see the world, not help light it on fire!" He protested.

"But you did." Kannan's voice broke just a little. "With every errand. Every word you carried between your captain and the shore. You didn't mean to. But it happened."

Tomas looked away. "Your people shouldn't have to choose between tradition and survival."

Kannan shook his head. "We always have. But this?" he gestured wildly to the smoke-stained skyline. "This is different. The stories are changing. We're not just fighting for our Gods or our trade. We're fighting not to forget ourselves. Do you get that?"

There was silence. Only the faint crackle of distant fire, the rustle of palm leaves, the low hum of a city unraveling.

"Yes," Tomas said finally, his voice hoarse. "Yes, I do."

Kannan exhaled, sharp and shaky. "Then don't choose like your captain. Don't stand beside him just because he found you a berth on his ship."

"I'm not," Tomas said. "I'm trying to choose better."

"Try harder," Kannan said. Then softer, almost a whisper: "Because if this turns, there won't be time left for second chances."

They stood there, caught in the smoke and the dusk, the line between them stretched tight and trembling. Far below, a drumbeat began. This time louder. Closer. No longer warning.

Calling.

That night, fire lit the sky.

No battle. Not yet. But houses near the spice docks were set alight. Not Portuguese ones. Local. Collateral in a brewing war of whispers.

Fighting broke out in alleys. One of the Portuguese guards was stabbed near the banyan tree. The body was dumped in a canal. A Nair warrior's corpse was later found on the sand, throat slit. No one claimed either. Everyone knew how both had met their end.

Da Gama doubled his watches. The Zamorin, sources said, consulted oracles. Tomas paced the deck, sleepless. He found Kannan staring out over the water.

"We can't stay," Tomas said.

"We?"

"Yes," he said.

Kannan shook his head. "It's not that simple."

"It never is. But we need to get them out. The prisoners. Before this becomes something no one can walk away from."

"They'll kill you for treason."

"Not if they don't know."

Kannan stared at him. "And after?"

Tomas met his eyes. "After? We find a different road."

They made their plan beneath the mango tree where Kannan once showed Tomas how to climb without sound. The tree stood in the yard of an abandoned spice godown, its branches gnarled like old hands, leaves still dusted with soot from distant fires. It was a place untouched by patrols, by foreign feet. A sanctuary of sorts, for scheming what could no longer be spoken aloud.

Three signal lanterns, one for ready, two for delay, three for go. A diversion near the harbour gates, set by a boy who sold betel leaves and knew every guard's lazy blink. Keys swapped for food during shift change, passed like secrets in a palmful of rice and dried mango.

Tomas scrawled the plan in charcoal on a strip of fabric, then burned it to ash. It would take luck. No. It would take more than luck. It would take resolve. And a reckoning neither of them dared name.

"Do you trust me?" Tomas asked.

Kannan didn't answer right away. He knelt, unwrapping a small pouch from his waist cloth. Inside: powdered ash mixed with tamarind bark. Used by temple dancers to darken their skin under stage light. He pressed it into Tomas's hand.

"Don't wear your boots," Kannan said, eyes steady. "They speak too loud."

In the hours before dawn, when even the sea seemed hushed and the stars above blinked uncertainly, they moved. Kannan went first, melting into the alleyways, slipping past shuttered stalls and sleeping cattle. He crept along the back walls of the harbour, barefoot, blending with shadows and old routines. Twice he paused as patrols passed. Portuguese soldiers in twos, their armour clinking faintly like wind chimes in fog.

Tomas waited by the edge of the grain yard. His face was streaked with ash, his breath slow, controlled. He followed two guards up the gangplank of the main vessel, walking behind them with a bucket and rag like a deck swab. Like he belonged. At the top, he gave a nod. The sleepy guard at post waved him through, barely looking up.

Down below, the hold was quiet. Too quiet. He crouched by the latch, heart pounding. One breath. Two. Then he slid the key into the lock.

The mechanism resisted. Old metal, warped by salt air. For a terrible moment, it held. Then: click. The door groaned open. Inside, the detained men stared at him with wary disbelief.

"Follow. Now," Tomas whispered. "Silently."

They slipped out one by one, Tomas leading, the fisherman bringing up the rear.

Outside, Kannan had started the diversion. A small clay pot filled with oil and wrapped in cloth burst near the gates, flames licking the base of a wooden barrel. Guards shouted. One blew a whistle.

In the confusion, the group moved like a shoal. Fast, fluid, vanishing into the fog-laced alleyways. They ran through ankle-deep water that tasted of salt and smoke, the city still thick with last night's fear. Behind them, shouts multiplied. A horn. Then a blade hissed past Tomas's shoulder, nicking the air with death.

Kannan ducked, grabbed Tomas's arm, and dragged him behind a stack of crates. Someone cried out. Then silence.

And then, footsteps retreating. Wrong direction. Misdirected.

The freed men didn't wait. They knew the streets, the corners, the names of gates that weren't marked on maps. Within moments, they were gone into the belly of the city, swallowed by its stubborn resistance.

By the time the sun pierced the horizon, throwing long shafts of firelight across the water, the harbour stank. Not of fish or brine, but of tension. The kind that clings to the skin. The kind that precedes blood.

Onboard the ships, tempers flared. Orders were barked. Accusations flew.

In the city, bells rang late, and low, and wrong. Not for prayer. Not for mourning. For reckoning.

And somewhere, beneath it all, a war had begun to breathe. Not as a beast. Not yet. But as a promise.

CHAPTER SIXTEEN

The Breath Before The Wave

The city of Calicut no longer breathed. It bristled.

Rumour moved quicker than men, slipping under doorways and through markets. They said the Portuguese had taken hostages. They said there had been a daring escape. They said there was a boy who walked invisible, and a foreigner who no longer served his flag. At the edge of every alley, eyes watched. Atop every temple step, the air crackled with incense and unrest.

Tomas and Kannan had not stopped running.

They slipped through broken lanes and over shuttered courtyards, weaving through the bones of the city like hunted ghosts. Tomas's face was still smeared with ash. Kannan's breathing was sharp and tight. The fishermen had been hidden away. Safe for now, but the city was closing in.

When they reached the eastern edge of the spice quarter, they found him waiting. The man in the indigo turban. He stood beneath the shadow of a charred pavilion, framed by hanging marigold garlands that no longer held colour. His red thread glinted once in the moonlight.

Tomas stopped short. "You again."

Kannan blinked. "You know him?"

Tomas nodded slowly. "I've met him twice. Once near the burned shrine. And once... before that, near the temple steps. He vanished both times. Like he was watching me."

The man smiled, the same inscrutable curve of the lips that had followed Tomas since that first meeting. "Not watching," he said quietly. "Waiting."

Kannan stared, his voice low and cautious. "Who are you?"

The man stepped forward, fingers brushing the burnt edge of a spice crate. "Someone who knew your father," he said, turning to Kannan. "And someone who made a promise long ago, to look after what he left behind."

Kannan's breath caught.

"He used to come here," the man went on, eyes softening. "To this very pavilion, when it was a rest stop for spice porters. He brought you once, barcly walking. You chewed on cardamom pods like they were treasure."

Kannan took a half-step back. "Why didn't you come sooner?"

"I did," the man replied. "But you didn't see me."

Tomas watched the exchange with a knot forming in his chest. The city's pulse pounded through the walls, echoing the war drums in his heart.

"What do you want from us?" he asked finally.

"Nothing," the man said. "But I offer something. A path forward. Before the city swallows you whole."

They moved quickly under the stranger's direction.

In a quiet warehouse near the docks, the man unfurled a small cloth map. It was hand-drawn, inked with precision, and marked with three symbols: a broken gate, a hidden jetty, and a shaded grove outside the city walls.

"This," he said, "is the only way you leave Calicut now. Da Gama will not forgive what you've done."

Tomas nodded grimly. "He already knows."

As if conjured by the thought, the harbour beyond the shutters erupted with shouts. The Portuguese flag fluttered violently above the foremast of *Sao Gabriel*, and on the upper deck, Da Gama stood, a storm given shape.

"They'll hang him," Kannan whispered.

"No," the stranger said, his voice quiet but firm."He's more useful alive for now. But when morning comes, your name will be spoken with curses on both shores."

Tomas turned to the map again. "We leave tonight."

The stranger gave him a sharp look. "You'll need distraction. The spice fire two lanes over will burn again.

Loud. Bright. Enough for your trail to vanish."

Kannan's eyes didn't move from the man. "Why are you helping us?"

He paused. "Because the ocean forgets names. But the land remembers. And you, boy... you were never meant to serve a flag."

In the pre-dawn hush, Tomas and Kannan moved like smoke.

The stranger had melted back into the folds of the city, as silently as he'd come. The signal would be lit by another loyal hand. One of the old guilds that hadn't forgotten the codes of the land.

Kannan wore a dark shawl wrapped tight around him, barefoot, with his mother's bead in one hand. Tomas moved with a sailor's stride but not a soldier's posture. They kept close to the lanes between fisher homes and temple courtyards, where only oil lamps flickered and cats prowled.

In the lower quarters, near the temple where lamps once lit a goddess's face, a basket of chilies caught fire. The blaze leapt high, red and orange like a second sunrise. Bells rang. Not sacred ones, but metal clappers used to warn of flood and riot. People poured into the streets. Not a mob.

Something older, stranger. A crowd that did not run, but turned inward.

Tomas and Kannan slipped through it like shadows between teeth. They reached the hidden jetty as smoke drifted like broken prayers across the water. A single canoe waited, oars already slick with river silt. No name, no flag. They pushed off just as voices roared down the embankment behind them.

Kannan turned once, toward the city that had raised him and betrayed him in equal measure. "Will it end?" he asked.

Tomas, hands tight on the oar, didn't answer. His chest felt too full of salt and shame. He had walked too many roads with no name. When they crossed the river bend, the city fell away. But the fire did not.

On the other side of the river, beneath a shroud of jungle silence, Tomas leaned back against the reeds, chest heaving. Kannan sat beside him, mud streaked on his palms.

"You were right," Tomas said finally. "About what?"

"You can't walk both roads when they split."

Kannan looked up at the sky. "Then let's not walk. Let's make a new one."

And in that pause, in the breath between dawn and daylight, two runaways; one from empire, the other from fate, looked out toward a land unclaimed by either.

The war had not ended.

But something older had begun.

From the deck of *Sao Gabriel,* Da Gama watched the shore with eyes full of steel. The captured fisherman had vanished. The city had answered with silence and stone. And his own man, a sailor who once cleaned blood off deck railings without flinching, had chosen the shore. The escape still stung. A sharp insult to his command. One of his own men had turned. A boy with calloused feet and salt in his voice had played the city better than any diplomat.

A first officer approached. "No word yet."

Da Gama's jaw clenched. "Then burn the silence."

By his order, two skiffs were lowered. Sailors armed and ready. A signal was fired into the sky. The response was chaos. Da Gama's voice was low, bitter. "We sail soon. But not empty-handed. Next time, we take what's owed. With steel."

But as the skiffs rowed toward the smouldering jetty, and the last flames of the decoy fire licked the blackened sky, something in the air shifted.

Calicut, wounded but not bowed, stirred with a memory older than empire. The streets that had once opened for merchants and kings now closed in defence of silence. The old guilds whispered again. The watchers in the temple shadows tightened their cloaks. And in courtyards where jasmine once bloomed, mothers told their children not tales of saints or spice. But of a boy who vanished with the dawn and a foreigner who chose the shore.

No proclamation would ever capture it. No scroll would bear their names. But a story had rooted itself into the soil. Of rebellion, of escape, of defiance. And when Da Gama's ships finally pulled from shore, sails swollen with salt and fury, the city did not mourn. It remembered.

For days afterward, the scent of river mud and ash hung in the air.

And far from the harbour, in the hush of forest beyond reach, two boys watched the sunrise over a land they did not yet understand. Not sailors. Not slaves. Not warriors. Just two names, no longer carried by wind or war, but by will. And behind them, the city exhaled. Scarred, but not silenced.

Epilogue

The Aftermath of Silence

The years that followed Calicut's darkest hour became the stories of rivers and stars, of men who vanished in the haze of rebellion and those who clung to flags that no longer fluttered in the same winds.

Tomas, once a sailor bound by the orders of a foreign flag, found his way not across endless seas but deep into the heart of the land. He and Kannan drifted into the embrace of the jungles beyond the city, taking only the knowledge of their shared escape and the quiet promise of the stranger's map. What they became in those years, no one truly knew.

There were whispers of a wandering warrior and his silent companion who spoke little but acted with fierce resolve. Some said they took to the hills, living as legends and teaching the old ways to those who would listen. Others claimed they carved their names into the very earth itself. So deeply that the land would bear their legacy long after empires crumbled.

But in truth, no man could trace their footsteps after that final night. Tomas never sought redemption. The sea had tried to take him too many times, and the shore, with its promise of freedom and danger, became his place of reckoning. His was a journey of escape. But one that, over time, shaped him into something more than the sum of his betrayals.

Kannan, too, was forever changed. He had walked in the shadow of an empire and then stepped into the unknown, the child of war now a man of the land. But it was the memory of his father that kept him tethered to the soil, to the fires of the people he'd once left behind. They say he could be found in quiet corners of the spice quarter, speaking in hushed tones to traders who'd once been loyal to Da Gama. But Kannan no longer needed the approval of empire. His words, now full of fire, carried the strength of his father's resolve.

The stranger with the indigo turban never came to see them again. Some say he had simply vanished, a figure woven into the very fabric of the city. His purpose fulfilled, he left no trace but the red thread that tugged at their memory. Yet it was his quiet presence that had given Tomas and Kannan the courage to choose their own path. He was more than a guide. Hhe was the thread of fate itself, weaving lives together in silence and leaving them to unravel as they willed.

And as for Da Gama, he sailed on. Wounded, but relentless. His ambitions, now tarnished by betrayal, stretched far beyond Calicut. But the man who had once wielded imperial power in his grasp found himself adrift, a man without a shore. The flames that had once burned so bright beneath his feet were now nothing more than embers, and the name of Vasco da Gama, the conqueror, began to fade from the pages of history. His ships would continue their course, yes. But the winds that pushed them forward were no longer the winds of glory. They were the winds of regret.

Years later, when the smell of spices and salt still lingered on the air, and the earth seemed to hold its breath once more, the people of Calicut would remember the quiet escape that had shattered the stillness of their city. It was said that in the final days before their departure, Tomas and Kannan stood at the edge of the river one last time, watching the sun rise over the land they would never truly leave.

The sea, a dark and unforgiving beast, still called to them. But it was no longer their master.

And the city, scarred by war and whispers, would find its new heart in the hands of those who had not bowed to flags, not bled for empires, but stood tall for the land they had been born to. It would

no longer be a city of conquerors. It would be a city of those who chose to live, to resist, and to remember.

For in the end, it wasn't the war that mattered. It wasn't the blood that had been spilled, or the betrayals that had been made. What mattered was the land, and those who walked it. Those who dared to step off the roads that others had paved for them, and make their own way.

Tomas and Kannan had left their mark on Calicut, not in the fire of battle, but in the quiet of the night, in the way they refused to be owned by any flag, by any king, or by any man. Their names, though never spoken aloud, had taken root deep in the soil of the city. And with time, as the dust settled and the rivers flowed on, they became something more than just two runaways.

They became a legend.

— END —

9 798899 295331